Finding Carla

To Michelle

Best Wishes

Finding Carla

LESLEY ANNE BROWN

First published in 2023 by Wrate's Publishing

ISBN 978-1-7393758-6-7

First Edition

Edited and typeset by Wrate's Editing Services

www.wrateseditingservices.co.uk

Cover design by Rachel Middleton

A CIP catalogue record for this book is available from the British Library.

To my beautiful granddaughter,
Mia Jane Brown

Posthumous Pieces

These pieces are called "posthumous,"
Not because I am "dead";
Unborn, that is forever impossible,

But because *they* are,
Which is inevitable.

They are tombstones,
A record of living intuitions
Which, embalmed in relative terminology,
Are well and truly dead.

WEI WU WEI

SENTIENT PUBLICATIONS, LLC

First Sentient Publications edition, 2004

Reprinted in the United States by Sentient Publications, by arrangement with Hong Kong University Press, Hong Kong.

Grateful acknowledgment is made for permission to use Matt Errey's editorial notes.

Cover design by Kim Johansen, Black Dog Design
Book design by Anna Bergstrom

Library of Congress Cataloging-in-Publication Data

Wei, Wu Wei.
Posthumous pieces / Wei Wu Wei.-- 1st ed.
p. cm.
ISBN 1-59181-015-9
1. Asia--Religion. 2. Spiritual life. I. Title.
BL1033 .W43 2004
202--dc22

2003018025

Printed in the United States of America

10 9 8 7 6 5 4 3 2 1

SENTIENT PUBLICATIONS
A Limited Liability Company
1113 Spruce St.
Boulder, CO 80302
www.sentientpublications.com

Contents

Part II: Sentience

Part III: The Conceptual Universe - 1

Acknowledgements

Chapter 4: "The Nonsense of 'Life' and 'Death,'" Chapter 32: "I, Noumenon, Speaking," Chapter 99: "The Supreme Vehicle Is . . .," and Chapter 95: "True-Seeing," are reprinted by kind permission of the Editor of *The Mountain Path* (April and October 1966, January and July 1967), Sri Ramanasramam, Tiruvannamalai, S. India. Chapter 34: "Why Are We Unaware Of Awareness?" Chapter 60: "The Buddha Taught," and Chapter 92: "Whole-Mind," are reprinted by kind permission of the Editor of *The Middle Way* (August and November 1966, and November 1967), 58 Eccleston Square, London, S.W.I. The following have appeared in *Être Libre*, 21 rue Père Dedeken, Brussels, Belgium: "Je Ne Suis Pas, Donc Je Suis," "La Notion Illusoire d'Une Realité," "L'Illusion d'Être," "La Pure Perception," "Suivant le Soufisme," "Vivre Libre," "Ce Que Nous Sommes," "La Fausse Route," "Pourquoi Il n'y a pas de Mort," "Le Pseudo-Mystère du Temps" (August and December 1960, September and December 1961, September 1962, September and December 1964, September 1965, September 1966, and June 1967).

Foreword

I LOVE Wei Wu Wei. In an age when Enlightenment is being crudely packaged and sold like toothpaste, WWW demonstrates that deft touch which is so essential when dealing with the absurdity of trying to express the inexpressible. As a fellow toiler in these fields, I very much appreciate his response to the challenge.

Whereas I start my talks about this impossible subject with the admonition that nothing I say is the Truth, Wei Wu Wei begins by stating that what he is saying is by its very nature relative and thus utterly and completely dead. He likens his pointers, his relative teaching concepts, to tombstones. And so his utterances, his Posthumous Pieces, are removed from the lofty precincts of scripture and thus, like tombstones, are propped up amongst the weeds.

In fact, even the conceptual grave Wei Wu Wei dug was largely neglected for several years. His publisher, the Hong Kong University Press, stopped visiting and bringing flowers so to speak, and this book along with his others went out of print.

Some years ago, when I was the publisher of the Advaita Press, I contacted the HK University Press about reprinting Wei Wu Wei's books. Unfortunately, at that time it seemed there were only about ten of us worldwide with sufficient interest to actually BUY such arcane treatments of the non-dual teachings. The Advaita Press ultimately lacked the resources to undertake the project. In the intervening years, thanks in large part to the popularity of the non-dual Teachings of Ramesh Balsekar which are deeply rooted in Wei Wu Wei's, the subject experienced a resurgence. Now with the number of interested readers soaring well into the dozens, Connie Shaw and her Sentient Publications stands to lose only her socks, not her complete shirt, with this undertaking.

What you hold in your hands is a very highly distilled liquor . . . nearly 200 proof. In fact, it is so potent that it is more in the order of a solvent than an intoxicant. It is capable of dissolving the illusion of separateness, the false notion that we are limited to these body-mind organisms, these appearances in Consciousness that upon investigation are revealed to have no independent existence. It points to the fanciful nature of space-time and once this is apperceived (understood at a level more fundamental than the intellect) fully and completely, no further illusion is possible.

Like all great sages, Wei Wu Wei is not in the business of helping you attain Enlightenment. He knows you have no more substance than the shadow on the wall. Shadows on the wall cannot become Enlightened. He says, "Enlightenment" does not exist phenomenally at all, and "we" cannot have it—because it is what-we-are! His role in the fictional drama of life is to scream into the darkness about the true nature of What IS . . . the eternal, intemporal moment. It matters not if your preferred Teacher/Teaching calls it Consciousness, Heart, Mind, Love, God, Intemporality, What IS, Tao, Source, Beloved, Noumenon or a thousand other names . . . all are pointers to this one immutable Truth that is ALL that exists and from which you could not possibly be separate.

Wei Wu Wei and possibly this book may be the vehicle for "your" apperception to occur . . . though the wonderful irony is that if it does . . . who will remain to care?

Enjoy!

WAYNE LIQUORMAN
Ibiza, Spain
September 23, 2003

Apologia

APOLOGIES ARE offered for the all too evident inadequacy of the relative expression represented by these pieces.

Interpretation of the ever-present understanding, universally available, with what appears as patience, consistence, and pertinacity, is attributable to what is known as *wei wu wei,* which is a Taoist symbol implying functioning which is non-volitional, spontaneous, ineluctable and, as such, totally impersonal.

But its expression in the language of relativity thereby becomes personal, and the relative responsibility must fall entirely on whatever phenomenal "editor" may have been obliged to undertake it.

Preface

If we clearly apperceive the difference
Between direct apprehension in Whole-mind
And relative comprehension by reasoning
In mind divided into subject-and-object,
All the apparent mysteries will disappear.

For that will be found to be the key
Which unlocks the doors of incomprehension.

The Supreme Illusion

I

Who could there be to be born, to be lived, to be killed?

What could there be to be brought into existence or to be taken out of existence?

Where could there be a "space" in which objective existence could be extended?

When could there be a "time" during which objective existence could have duration?

These notions, so queried, belong to whoever has never profoundly considered these facile and conditioned assumptions, for all are conceptual images in mind, the supposed factuality of which is as imaginary as any mirage, hallucination, or dream, and all of which are experienced as both factual and actual.

But *the supreme illusion* is not that of the incidence of "birth," "life," and "death" as such, but that of there being any objective entity to experience these conceptual occurrences.

The *accessory illusion* is that of spatial and temporal extension subject to which the supreme illusion of entity is rendered possible and without which no "entity" could appear to suffer any experience whatever.

II

In the absence of the related and interdependent concepts of "space" and of "time" no element of the apparent universe could be conceived, could be cognised or apparently experienced, and no "entity" could be imagined in order to cognise or experience any such element.

Therefore there cannot be any factual entity to be born, to be "lived," or to be "killed," nor any factual object to be brought into existence or taken out of existence.

And it follows that all phenomena are only such, i.e. appearance in mind, perceived and cognised by mind itself, by means of the dichotomy of division into subject and object, and the resulting process of reasoning by the comparison of mutually dependent and opposing counterparts which constitutes the process of conceptualisation.

III

The implied Unicity, the totality of undivided mind, is itself a concept of its own division or duality, for relatively—relativity being relative to what itself is—it cannot be conceived or known at all.

All that could ever be known about it is simply that, being

Absolute, it must necessarily be devoid of any kind of objective existence whatever, other than that of the totality of all possible phenomena which constitute its relative appearance.

IV

During the two-and-a-half millennia of recorded history none of the sages has been able to transmit further or other representation of what apparent sentient-beings are in relation to the apparent universe in which they appear to be spatially and temporally extended. Religious elaboration of its own metaphysical basis, however comforting it may be, factually can only confuse the issue; but this does not mean that such elaboration is in any degree more or less false or more or less true in itself, relatively regarded, than any other speculation, but only that it must necessarily belong, however apparently spiritual, to the conceptual universe in which it inheres.

On the basis of this understanding the way should be clear for direct apperceiving of what each of us is and what all of us are as apparent sentient-beings; for without such necessary clearance, which is the negation of all the positive nonsense which holds us in supposed "bondage," we are like lost children in a conceptual forest of our own imagining.

Few people are likely to read these lines who are not seeking fulfillment, but fulfillment needs no seeking, and seeking will always maintain the apparent absence of fulfillment. If the imaginary forest has been cleared we have only to look in order to apperceive what, when, and where we are, that it is not what we *know,* but what "I AM," and that unborn, unliving, undying, it is here and now and forever.

Non-Being

Unextended conceptually in "space,"
Unprotracted conceptually in "time,"
Formless, therefore, and without duration,
Unborn, therefore, and undying,
Eternally we are as I.

PART I

Time

The Seeker is the found,
The found is the seeker,
As soon as it is apperceived
That there is no Time.

1 ·- Taking Time by the Forelock

NEARLY EVERYONE seems to accept time as though it existed absolutely, for indeed, almost always, everything is discussed and analysed in a time-context as though that were the *indisputable* foundation of all that is known.

The foundation, of course, it is, but how can it be regarded as indisputable? Has anyone ever produced any scrap of evidence of its objective existence—except the fact that everything depends on its existence, which is very precisely *une petition de principe* or begging the question?

Therefore to argue about the factuality of "things" as such, all subject to duration, without considering the validity of this "duration" on which they all entirely depend, would seem to be a singular lacuna in the logic of any such discussion. We must surely admit that until the validity of apparent "duration" is established the validity of whatever may depend on it cannot either be established or denied. It is the primary factor, and should have precedence over all else.

Discussing something whose existence is totally dependent on something else for whose existence no evidence has been adduced, or indeed can be adduced, apart from the supposed something under discussion that is dependent upon it, is indeed a performance of some futility! And what current religious or metaphysical discussion does not come into this category?

"Time"—and, of course, "space" from which it is inseparable—is basic to all phenomena, for without extension in duration and in volume they cannot have any apparent existence at all.

On examination "time" and "space" will be found to have no objective existence otherwise than as a conceptual structure in mind, an assumed background without which no phenomenon could appear. "Time" and "space," therefore, must be entirely subjective. Closer examination will reveal that they represent a further dimension of measurement (or dimension), conceptually an all-inclusive super-volume constituting what is implied by the term "subjectivity" itself.

Metaphysically expressed, we may say that I-noumenon manifest objectively what I am, in three directions of measurement, by means of a fourth or super-volume which is interpreted sensorially by divided-mind as what is known as "space-time."

If objectively "space-time" does not exist as any "thing" perceptible or cognisable, that must be because it can only be an expression of the non-objectivity which is perceiving and cognising, and that is what we are.

What then is "space-time"? It may tentatively be defined as the super-volume from which we observe, interpreted in a tri-dimensional universe as *extension,* by means of the consecutive duration of that apparent three-dimensional universe.

The "past" is a memory,
The "future" is a supposition,
The "present" is passed before we can apprehend it.*
The only "present" therefore is *presence* and must necessarily be what we are.
Such *presence,* then, is inevitably outside time and must be "intemporality."

---

* The processes of perception and conception are complicated and require a lapse of time for their completion.

2 · What Space-Time Is

I

WE CAN conceive infinity, vaguely perhaps, as unlimited space, and intemporality as unlimited time, both continuing "forever"; but, try as we may, we are unable to conceive the absence of space and the absence of time, and we have no words for these conceptual absences.

The term "eternity," perhaps, should denote an absence of duration which we are unable actually to conceive, but in fact whenever used it merely implies the opposite—"time without end." "Outside space and time" is a vague expression, of poetical character, and "spaceless" and "timeless" have no significance that is capable of visualisation.

It is the absence of a concept for a condition in which neither space nor time exists that is significant, for it must necessarily imply that *existence as such* is dependent on the concept of space-time. It is, of course, evident that this is the case, since all phenomena must be extended spatially and appear to have duration in order to be perceived, but the absence of these terms proves that we have in fact always known it.

II

The inconceivability of the absence of space-time, the fact that it cannot be thought in the sense of visualised, has a still more profound significance, since nothing objectifiable can be inconceivable.

What, then, is non-objectifiable? Surely any "thing," any kind of object whatsoever is imaginable? There cannot be anything at all that is *not* objectifiable, for any and every thing imaginable is thereby conceived in imagination.

What, then, could be inconceivable, what in fact is and must be inconceivable? Only that which is conceiving is itself inconceivable, for only what is conceiving cannot, when conceiving, conceive itself.

It might be maintained that what conceives might conceive itself as an imaginary object, like any other object, in consecutive duration, but conceiving as such, while conceiving, cannot conceive its own conceiving—any more than an eye can see its own looking. Therefore whatever is factually inconceivable can only be the conceiving itself which cannot cognise its own act of cognition.

This demonstrates the dialectic validity of the insight whereby we may apperceive that absence of space-time must necessarily be what we are who cannot conceive it.

It must be evident that what we are is "conceiving"—for what else could be conceiving what we conceive? And, if there is a phenomenal absence which we cannot conceive, that *absence* must necessarily be our own absence as what is conceiving.

The phenomenal absence of space-time, being inconceivable, must therefore be our own phenomenal absence as what is conceiving, and—since we cannot conceive our own absence—we must be what space-time is, and space-time must be what noumenally we are.

And that no doubt explains why all that we are, both phenomenally and noumenally, was termed "mind" by the great Masters of China.

Note: We may assume also that this explains why so very few people are willing to face up to the problem of space-time, why nearly all fight shy of it, decline to discuss it, and just accept it as something inevitable, whether philosophers, the religious, or those who seek "enlightenment." Yet surely anyone can see how vitally important it must be, that nothing can be finally understood while that remains unexplained, for it is obvious that whatever is subject to extension in space and to successional duration could not be veritable in itself. The study of space-time in physics may also be the key to the startling fact that so many of the greater physicists have found themselves on or over the borders of metaphysics, and have been brave enough to say so.

3 ·⁓ *Eight Words*

Objective existence is mythical,
Non-objective existence is absolute.

Note:

Objective existence is phenomenal—appearance only,
Non-objective existence is unaware of existing,
And it is phenomenally incognisable.

Objective existence is figuration in mind,
Non-objective existence only "exists" in such mind,
Cognising everything except what is cognising.

Objective mind is self-elaboration in space-time,
Non-objective mind, phenomenally void, knows neither.

By whom is this being said?
By mind attempting to see itself—and not succeeding.
Why? As space-time "it" appears as "void,"
Intemporally "it" cannot cognise what is cognising.

"Dying" is dying to phenomenality: "birth" is being born to phenomenality, i.e. to perceiving and—later—to conceiving.

That is why neither exists as such.

4 · The Nonsense of "Life" and "Death"

WHAT DIFFERENCE could there be between "living" and "dying"? "Living" is only the elaboration in sequential duration of what otherwise is known as "death."

When What-we-are functions, extending in three apparent spatial dimensions and another interpreting them as duration, together known as "space-time," there is what we know as "living." When that process ceases we are no longer extended in sequential duration, we are no longer elaborated in "space," "space-time" is no more and the apparent universe dis-appears.

Then we say we are "dead."

But as what we are we have never "lived," and we cannot "die."

Where could "we" live? When could "we" die? How could there be such things as "we"? "Living" is a spatial illusion, "dying" is a temporal illusion, "we" are a spatio-temporal illusion based on the serial interpretation of dimensional "stills" or "quanta" cognised as movement.

Only the concepts of infinity and intemporality can suggest intellectually a notion of what we are as the source and origin of appearance or manifestation.

5 ·– *Karma and Rebirth—A Dialogue*

Morning!

Hullo! Want something?

Yes. Tonic.

Well?

All said and done, what *are* "karma" and rebirth?

Little to be said *and nothing to be* done *about it.*

Very well, let's have the little.

"Karma" means "action" and the result of it. Find me someone to act and we'll discuss his action, find me someone to be born and we'll discuss his rebirth.

So they are both hooey?

Better when spelled with a "w" in front.

Never been a "who?" and never will be?

Only in a conceptual space-time context.

As an appearance in mind?

Any kind of dream, dreamed by a dreamer.

Good, but in that case?

Ask someone who thinks he knows about all that.

Who does?

Any dreamed phenomenon who is being dreamed and doesn't know it. Usually have letters after their names.

All their apparent actions?

The volitional ones.

There are two kinds?

Yes and No: spontaneous, and accompanied by a will-impulse.

The volitional element creates "karma"?

How could it not?

And that leads to rebirth?

The "re" is tautological. Appearance occurs every split-second.

Ksana in Sanscrit?

Any language you like.

I refer to Sanscrit because those boys knew about all that.

Scholars like to think so, at least.

Why do they do that?

Justify their "karma," like the rest of us.

But, without the volitional element, what is it?

What Sages appear to do. Ask them.

Can't we do it too?

We "can" not , but it may occur.

Nevertheless we do it?

It is not a "deed."

Why?

Because no one "does" it.

Then what is it?

A do-ing.

Which is?

Functioning. You like Sanscrit: "prajña" is that.

And "prajña"?

"Dhyana," the principal of functioning, looking for itself.

And "dhyana"?

Whatever says it. "Prajña," functioning, is the saying.

And the two of them?

There aren't two.

Well the one then?

There isn't one.

Then what is it?

Whatever you are, you ass!

But that?

Not that! *You tell me, for a change.*

This, then?

Better, but still—no.

Nothing whatever?

No, no.

Then what?

The absence of that: "nothing" is a negative "something"; and you would still appear to be as an objective entity.

I must be total absence?

Since you are total presence.

6 ·⁃ Space

THAT WHICH is not extended in space can have no perceptual existence, for the concept of "existing" denotes and requires spatial extension.

That is the explanation of Hui Neng's statement: "From the beginning not a thing is," i.e. "No 'thing' has ever existed," for there has never been such a thing as "space" other than as a concept in mind (which we are) which renders possible the notion of appearance.

Note: It should hardly be necessary to treat of Space independently of Time, for they are not separate—Time, as we have seen, being a spatial concept interpreted as duration. Therefore what has been said regarding Time is applicable to Space and only requires the necessary verbal adjustment. It may be said that whereas treating the space-concept directly is more radical, treating it via the time-concept may be an approach more readily appreciated. Ultimately the concept whose demolition must result in understanding is that which is known as "Space-time."

❧

Nothing could be more obviously imagined than "space" and "time," yet people assume them to be permanent and objective realities! Basic they may be, but as the basis of an elaborate dimensional fiction.

7 ·⁃ Come to Think of It . . .

HUANG PO on "time": "If there's never been a single thing—past, present, and future are meaningless. . . . *Full* *understanding of this must come before they (you) can enter the Way*" (Blofeld, p. 110).*

One must be tireless in pointing out that unless we (each of us) face up to the apparent problem of what "time" is we shall never see the way things are—other than phenomenally, nor shall we understand what we are apparently doing in this apparent universe. Taking "time" for granted—as everyone seems determined to do—is searching blindfold for an open door.

So, "past, present, and future are meaningless"—because from the beginning "there's never been a single thing": phenomenally indispensable, noumenally—just meaningless. And *vice versa* one may say "Things are meaningless—because there's never been a past, present or future."

Let us analyse this proposition. "Things" are wholly dependent on "time" (past, present, and future) for the extension that renders them perceptible as "things," and were they not perceptible how could they be "things"? Things, therefore, are only the perceptibility or the perceiv-ing of "things."

And "time" is wholly dependent on "things" (objects perceived) in order that it may be cognised and conceptualised

---

* *"Entering a way"* implies movement in duration, and Huang Po has just stated that "past, present, and future are meaningless"! There must be a misunderstanding? When one points out that "the Way" is the "philological" translation of "Tao," which that word can and does sometimes mean colloquially, but which—as is often pointed out here—it does *not* mean metaphysically, it will be seen that Tao is a synonym for Dharmakaya, Bhutatathata, Buddha-mind, Noumenon, so that the sentence implies *"Full understanding of this must come before you can re-become (or actualise) what-you-are."*

as "time," for without objects perceived, being perceived, about to be perceived, there could be no "time"—for "time" is only the cognition of "things in duration."

"Time" (duration), therefore, must be inherent in objects, inseparable from objects, an aspect of objects, as "space" must—to which the same factors apply—so that "time" and "space" must both be inherent in perceiv-ing.

It follows that all phenomena are the perceiv-ing of phenomena, and that their extension and duration is inherent in the mechanism whereby perceiv-ing appears to occur, the dualist mechanism of noumenon phenomenalising noumenality.

Does this not demonstrate the correctness of the metaphysical intuition common to Buddhism, Vedanta, and Sufism?

There is only perceiv-ing: all else is void of noumenality—the eye that cannot see what is looking.

❧

The "future" is a dream. The "past" is recollection of a dream. The "present" is an unlikely hypothesis.

What, then, is left? Must I say it? Why, Intemporality, of course!

It never was any "where" or at any "time" but Here and Now, and Here and Now it will be forever.

Ed. note: The Huang Po quotes are from John Blofeld's "The Zen Teaching of Huang Po."

8 · "The Truth of Ch'an"

"SUDDEN (INSTANTANEOUS) Enlightenment" is the essential teaching of the Supreme Vehicle, chiefly represented by Ch'an, and in this Intemporality is necessarily implied, since it is nowise dependent on duration. But it is not generally realised that this implication must also necessarily include the negation of the validity of the notion of "time" as the *sine qua non* of phenomenal manifestation.

It follows that even Ch'an (and, of course, Zen) must make nonsense as long as the concept of "time" is retained as the basic element of conceptualisation therein. It follows also that the implied notion of "space," whose duration it measures, must be apperceived as being part of the mechanism of objectivisation, and rejected.

"Time" may then be re-cognised as being a further direction of measurement beyond those by which we constitute our phenomenal universe in "space," interpreted—since our psychic apparatus is only equipped to cognise via three—as the *duration* of tri-dimensional volume.

The basic doctrine of Ch'an, and of Zen, being the immediate or timeless character of awakening to what-we-are, the comprehension of "space-time" must necessarily be integral in its apprehension. Such instantaneity being the essential teaching, "intemporality" must be that also—for each is an aspect of the other.

As long as we continue to remain oblivious of this essential and primordial factor, accepting it as not only actual but factual, is it reasonable to suppose that we shall awaken to what Huang Po called "the Truth of Ch'an"?

Note: The phrase "The Truth of Ch'an" is translated for us by John Blofeld in his profound and brilliant translation of Huang Po as "The Truth of Zen," but poor Huang Po had not the good fortune ever to have heard of Zen or of what his Japanese neighbours were to make of the teaching of his masters and of his own, however important and valuable that may be. Do we refer to the Old Masters of Italian painting by the name of a subsequent school in another land?

9 ·- Nameless and I

DARKNESS IS only apparent absence of light, otherwise there is no such thing: the word can only indicate that absence, for such itself has no kind of presence.

Death is only apparent absence of life, otherwise there is no such thing. The word only indicates the absence of the presence of life. To think of death as such is senseless. There can never be any such presence, for phenomenally it is only an absence.

"Life" is a concept extended in space-time, and as such it is only an image in mind. Conceptually also it is the absence of "death" which—as we have seen—is the absence of "life."

Evidently, therefore, there is no such factuality as "life," nor any such factuality as "death." Nor can there be any factual entity such as a "liv-er" of life or a "dy-er" of death.

But there is a phenomenal manifestation called "liv-*ing*" and another called "dy-*ing*," both extended in a space-time concept, and these latter have a direct relation to what we are.

Such relation, however, can never be evident as long as we adhere to the notion of "life" and "death" as factual existences.

What we are is manifested in the spatio-temporal appearance of "liv-*ing*," and dis-appears in that of "dy-*ing*," but in order to apperceive what this is it is necessary to discard the notions of the "liv-ing" of a "life" and the "dy-ing" of a "death"—for what-we-are neither "lives" nor "dies."

We must cast both into the dustbin of futile concepts, and so leave ourselves in our presence, which cannot be subject to any kind of phenomenal extension, either spatial or temporal, or to any kind of sensorial objectivisation whatever.

What, then, does this imply? It implies the abandonment of split-mind as an instrument of apperceiving, for such abandonment leaves us inevitably in our wholeness—also "holiness" and "health" which are the same word—and as such we are noumenal integrality,—neither positive nor negative, immanent nor transcendent—nameless and I.

❧

We have to split mind in order to dream,
We have to split mind in order to live and to die,
Let us stop splitting mind—and stay whole!

One might be lonely in the absence of "other"?
Unless "one" were "all" there could be no "one,"
Unless "all" were "one" there could be no "all."

10 ~ Sequentia Fugit

I

THE FUTURE should not be envisaged as some "thing" that is awaiting us, any more than the past should be envisaged as some "thing" that is gone-for-ever.

Neither has either come or gone, is either to-come or to-go, because neither is a "thing" at all or has any objective existence whatever.

Both are what we call "the present" which to us only appears to exist as an imaginary line separating two temporal states which we are obliged to experience sequentially. They are just *Presence,* which has for aspects "past" and "future" as a coin has head and tail.

II

The future is already "now," has never been anywhen else, and will never go elsewhen. It does not exist as a "future" at all, nor will it ever exist as a "past." It is entirely here now, always has been and will be "forever"—in a time-context.

It is the "time-context" which is imagined, according to which events are experienced in sequence. "Sequence" appears to "fly" and we call it "Tempus." Nothing else suffers any kind of displacement in Mind.

Note: "Mind" here refers to the integrality of mind, whose division into subject and object produces relativity, "future" and "past" being relative concepts.

III

The centre of infinity is in all "places,"
And I am the centre of all infinity.
The centre of intemporality is at all "times,"
And I am the centre of all intemporality.

Therefore here-and-there, near-and-far,
Are measurements from where-I-am,
And now-and-then, passed and to come,
Are measurements of my presence-and-absence,
From my eternal centre.

11 ⁓ The Dying-Dream

WHERE THE so-called problem of "death" is concerned it would seem reasonable to start by enquiring "What is there to die?"

One obvious answer might be "Whatever was born." Another should perhaps be "Only what is called 'matter' can be subject to either birth or death." Thus these answers are inseparable.

"Death" and "birth" are inseparable also; that is to say they are only *apparently* separated as a consequence of the conceptual extension of the concept of "matter" in space and duration.* But that, absolutely all that, is ideation.

Apart from ideation, what could there be to be born or to die? The living-dream and the dying-dream are not essentially different from the sleeping-dream—since all are ideation in mind. "Waking" and "sleeping" are a pair of relative and interdependent counterparts, inseparable and only negatively veridical—veridical in mutual negation.

12 ⁓ Presence in the Present

I

"THE PRESENT" only appears to exist relatively—in relation with what is past and with what is to come. It cannot have

* "The cause, displaced in time and space, appears as its effect." (The Nirvana Prakarna of the Maha Ramayana). Death, therefore, appears as a space-time effect of birth.

any independent existence as a "present."*

"Being present in the present" is a positive concept and as such must constitute bondage, whereas "being absent from a present" is a negative concept and should constitute liberation.

Since it must be the absence of presence that perceives a "present," to the supposedly present what is perceiving must be absent.

Therefore my "being present in the present" is phenomenally an absence.

II

No present moment could be perceived, since it must be in the "past" before the complicated process of perception could be completed—therefore our notion of "the present" could only exist in a "past."

But a "future" and a "past" only appear to exist in relation with a supposed "present." All three temporal concepts are mutually interdependent, so that there can be no basis for any of them.

The absence of a "present" thereby implies total phenomenal absence—the existential absence of any universe whatsoever, whereas my phenomenal absence, perceiving itself as a presence in a phenomenal "present," *must necessarily be the noumenality of all phenomena.*

---

* A concept of a self-existing "present" should inevitably imply noumenal intemporality, timeless non-objectivity, which could not be applicable in any phenomenal context.

13 ·– Analytical Observations Concerning Time

I

I DO NOT know whether advances in the accuracy of mathematical instruments have allowed scientists to calculate the duration of the time-lag between the perception of a supposed object and its completed conception and recognition by memory as whatever such object may be said to be. Each element in that process, whether visual, auditory, olfactory, gustatory, or tactile, is well-known, complicated, indeed elaborate, involving chemical changes in more than one set of cells, apart from the transmission of nerve-impulses, so that the final interpretation can only be a mnemonic structure in the psyche.

However considerable it may be, the importance of such duration is not of metaphysical interest, but merely the obvious fact that it must "exist" and must, relatively speaking, be considerable. It must therefore follow from this that if duration has objective existence whatever we psychically regard as "present" or "the present" must necessarily be well and truly in the past by the time we have become aware of its recognition as what we are conditioned by memory to think that it is.

What conclusions should we draw from this?

1. That what we regard as "the present" is in fact "the past" when we know it.

2. There is, therefore, no "present" that we can cognise as such:

3. In fact we are actually "living" in "the future" which we can never know as such until it is factually in "the past."

Should this be difficult to envisage, and since only the general circumstance is in question, the duration of the time-lag is unimportant, so that in order to envisage it easily we have only to imagine its duration, not as being too brief to be recognised by our senses but as lasting, let us say, for a familiar period such as ten minutes. So regarded, the situation should readily appear evident.

It seems to follow that our "present," having passed, must be purely conceptual as a presence, in fact just a notion in mind, and can have no factual existence whatever: *we can know no actual present.*

It follows, also, that since in the hypothesis of objective duration we are already living in the "future," without being aware of it, nothing we imagine that we do in the already passed "present" could have any effect whatever on the "future" in which we are already living, since whatever we think we are doing in this passed "present" must necessarily be "done" in the unalterable past when we do it! If it be the result of conceptions themselves resulting from already past conditions, whatever we think we do volitionally can no longer affect anything.

It may now be evident that analysis reveals that the notion of an objective "time," of duration as an existence independent of this which is conceiving it as such, makes nonsense of what we recognise as "living"? If the perfect subjectivity of the notion of "time" needed demonstration does not analysis readily reveal that so it must be?

Therefore is it not clear that we neither live in a "past" nor in a "future," and that our "present" is an image in mind like that of the Equator? "Time" is nothing objective to which we are subjected, but a measurement of our phenomenal extension in "space," integrated with the sensorial experience of what ultimately we are.

II

It is by means of apparent extension in "space" and a fourth directional measurement of that, experienced as duration, that "we" are able to experience phenomenally what noumenally we are.

As long as we objectify our spatial and temporal measurements, regarding them as independent of ourselves, it should be evident that we could never recognise ourselves noumenally, since it is that spatio-temporal framework, supposedly external to ourselves, which—subjected to that objective servitude—psychically holds us in captivity. It is in fact to the concepts of spatial and temporal extension that what noumenally we are appears to be bound phenomenally—for it is on space-time that all phenomenality depends. This "bondage" is conceptual, due to the objectivisation of what is subjective, thereby obscuring our noumenality.

Whether the required adjustment be difficult or easy, it must be evident that this is the essential reorientation necessary for release from what undoubtedly constitutes "samsara" as opposed to "nirvana," which—as we are taught—are not fundamentally either separate or different.

In what, then, does such reorientation consist, what is required in order to bring it about? The answer to this question seems to be that essentially we must cease to regard what conceptually we know as "space" and "time" as objective to what is conceiving them. That is to say that we are required to recognise that they are an aspect of ourselves, inseparable from whatever we are, and integral in our phenomenal manifestation. "Space-time" must cease to be a concept of something external on which our appearance depends, and instead must be apperceived as not anything cognisable but as an aspect of what is cognising.

What is cognising? We are; nothing could there be to cognise, and what is cognising could not be a "thing," i.e. an object of cognition. What we think of as "space-time" is incognisable: it is a theoretical proposition, an hypothesis like the "aether," psychically projected.

"Space-time" is a conception of what is so conceiving it in "space-time," and as such it could not have any kind of factuality. As an element of phenomenalisation, of the elaboration of our objective universe in mind, it is what we are—phenomenalising what we are, as are all our sensorial perceptions. It is not something we perceive but an element of what is perceiving. "Space-time" is nothing but we who are conceiving it.

III

All sensorial experience is experience of what we are, and cognition is our sixth sense. The sutras teach that sensorial experience, correctly understood, can lead directly to recognition of our noumenality and the Bodhisativas Avalokitesvara and Mañjusri lauded the auditory sense as the simplest way and that which they themselves had employed. The Buddha acquiesced but emphasised that all the senses are equal in that respect and that, whichever was applied, all conformed as one in *anuttara samyak sambhodi.* Such, therefore, was the teaching accepted as that of the Buddha by the great Masters of Ch'an at the highest period of its development.

But what experience is or could be more constant than that of space-time, and what experience could lead more directly back to its noumenal source and origin?

If we apprehend space-time as being non-objective, as a phenomenal functioning of our noumenal integrality, can it fail to dis-appear as an object in mind? In so-doing can its phenomenal disappearance leave our phenomenal identity intact? That must be forever impossible. Wherever "it" goes "we" go with it—for whatever "we" are it is. Objective extinction must comport subjective extinction, for no object can subsist without a subject, nor any subject without an object. Together their presence comports our presence as phenomenality, and together their absence must comport our phenomenal absence as noumenality. The presence of space-time is called "samsara," its absence is called "nirvana," and these are names for the positivity and negativity whose mutual negation is the only possible relative indication of what we could be.

Release from subjection to the concept of "time"—of duration in spatial extension—is the ultimate release, and it must be total. As such it is inevitably the most direct, for it is immediate. All other approaches are indirect, for they are via some medium *by means of which* the bonds which bind us to duration are broken, whereas phenomenal—which is temporal—experience experienced as duration, but apperceived as experience of what we are as I, must annihilate instantly all objective experience of temporality.

IV

The apparent "present" is each moment of awareness, resulting in mnemonic activity: it occurs in mind only. By the time cognition has occurred it belongs to the state termed the "past."

The "past" is mnemonic: it exists only in mind. It has passed and, temporally, is regarded as immutable although its mnemonic record varies and deteriorates.

The "future" is the suppositious state in which events must be assumed to have occurred, if occurrence has taken place, such events being subsequently cognised as being in the "present" although they must then necessarily have been in the "past."

Any movement that may have occurred can only have been mnemonic. Mind may have functioned in a manner that appears as sequence, but there has been no evidence of action exterior to the perceiving mind, or as having objective existence.

V

Therefore it would seem that no evidence can be adduced for the factual existence of the so-called "passage of time," so that the notions of "future," "present," and "past" are conceptual only, and should be recognised as a product of the process of relativity whereby the conceptual universe becomes apparent.

As such, "time" may also be regarded as a measurement of the three dimensions of volume by means of which the appearance of form can occur extended in what is termed "space," for without such measurement there could be no sequence in perception, and without sequential duration no object could appear to be perceived.

Perceiving is thus revealed as an apparently functional aspect of What-we-are as sentient beings. This—incidentally—is what the T'ang-dynasty Masters explained to us, using the Chinese equivalent of the Sanscrit term "prajña." This word represented to them an immanent or functional aspect of THIS or I, the symbol for which in Sanscrit was "Dhyana" or "Butatathata." The Taoists, at the time of Guatama the Buddha, referred to these two aspects of the process of sentient manifestation as Tao and Tê, and this mode of apprehension became the in-forming element of the Supreme

Vehicle later represented by Ch'an.

Note: Buddhistically speaking, need it be pointed out that all experience—pain and pleasure, the famous "suffering" (*dukha*) and its counterpart—could only be *experienced* in the sequence of duration, in the "horizontal" sequence of a "time"-dimension, and that without sequence, in the "vertical" dimension which cuts the horizontal in every split-second (*ksana*) of the former, there could not be duration, so that equanimity alone can subsist therein intemporally?

The sequential direction of measurement must constitute *samsaric* or split-mind, whereas the measurement at right-angles thereto represents *nirvanic* or whole mind. Therefore when subjective intemporality *(nirvana)* replaces objective temporality *(samsara)* the latter having been found to have no factuality, equanimity (an end to "suffering" and its counterpart) alone can obtain.

It may also be pointed out that, since we are demonstrably what "Time" subjectively is, metaphysically whatever we may be must necessarily be intemporal.

All objectivisation is seeing things in a time-sequence. Every such act, therefore, is a phantasy, a composition in temporality, an image of the non-existent.

That surely is why the bound objectivise and those who objectivise are bound. That also is why those who are free do not objectivise, and why those who do not are free.

14 ·– "The Essential Understanding Seems to Be . . ."

THE ESSENTIAL understanding seems to be that everything we can know appears to exist in "mind" and can have no other kind of existence whatever. If that has been apperceived as inevitable and factual, then we have to apperceive that this "mind" does not exist independently as such either. Why is that? The answer is almost absurdly simple: it is because "mind" is just a symbol for what we ourselves are, and therefore we cannot see it as an object independent of what is looking!

This so-called "mind" is just what is meant by the word "I" and, *when I turn outwards and objectify, "mind" divides into a duality of subject and its object.* This means that I create as an apparent object something other than I, so that "mind" is thereby split into "I-subject" and "you-object," "self" and "other." But I always remain as I, objectively void or devoid of objective existence. However, "you-object" are an apparently sentient being in "mind," and "you" start calling yourself "I" also—although you are factually only an object of Subject-I. Therefore I am always I, and "you" are always "you," but "you" can come back with that and say the same to "me"—since what I am as an object is "you" to you-as-I. Therefore we can say: "'We' are all the apparent objects of what mutually we all are, which, whoever says it, is always I."

In order to understand this more thoroughly it is necessary to see how it works. The process of objectifying is by splitting "mind," which as "I" remains whole and eternal (intemporal), into Duality which demonstrates what it is as "I" sensorially, which is relatively, by dividing its wholeness—which we can describe as "equanimity"—into contrasting elements, positive and negative, pleasure and pain, love and hate, and all the endless pairs of contrasting concepts. In order to do this, which is the conceptuality in which the universe appears in "mind" (now split), these images have to be extended in length, breadth, and height, which is called "volume," and in order to be perceptible they must be further extended by duration, which we call "time," which is a fourth direction of measurement interpreted as "lasting" or as being "horizontal" as opposed to "vertical," and which cuts the measurements of volume at right-angles, thus giving the illusion or impression of duration.

This space-time element, therefore, is nothing objective to ourselves as objects, is nothing independent to which we are subjected or "bound," but is part and parcel of our appearance, being our extension which renders us objectively perceptible to subjective perceiving. And our notion of "bondage" is just this illusion that we are independent entities subjected to temporality.

We know that what prevents us from knowing ourselves as "I" is this apparent temporality which enables the notion—that each of us is an independent "I"—to endure. These supposed "me"s only appear to exist because they appear to *last,* to endure, and if they did not, if they were not temporal, they would be intemporal which is what I AM whoever says it.

We have been taught that in order to know ourselves as "I" we must destroy the illusion that we exist as "me"s in duration, but we cannot destroy our "me"ness as long as we leave its duration as "me"ness objectively behind it, for the concepts are inseparable. They are not independent or different: they are elements of one another! If we could remove the notion of "me" for a moment, its "lasting" in "time" would still remain—and it would re-appear. Which it does. So "time" (duration) must go with it. We should apperceive what "time" is, that it is not an independent objectivisation but is an essential part of the objectivisation of our apparent "selves." The former, however, is insufficient as an independent operation for if the ego-concept be removed alone, the time-concept may remain, whereas if the time-as-an-object concept be removed the ego-concept which depends upon it, in which it extends as "lasting," must go with it. If it could not have duration, if it could not "last," it could not appear to be at all.

Therefore our problem is really only to apperceive that "time" could not be anything objective to "ourselves," but on the contrary must be, and clearly, demonstrably is an intrinsic element of what we are as phenomenal objects in mind.

Is not all this really very simple and obvious? As I—which is all that we could be—we are in-temporal and in-finite, for "time" and "space" are concepts by means of which what we are is objectivised in divided "mind" as phenomenal individuals through whom the whole objective universe appears so-extended and made perceptible sensorially. Those of us who are not satisfied to accept this phenomenal universe at its face-value and to make the best of our supposed "bondage" thereto, seek to apprehend what factually we are, and so to recover our intemporality which, as I, we have never lost. We make a lot of fuss about it, and let ourselves be led up the garden path by well-meaning, mostly religious, sages and prophets in the most abstruse and intricate manner conceivable, expounded in ancient metaphor and jargon of all sorts and descriptions, and all with remarkably mediocre results! Yet is it not in fact comparatively simple and obvious?

It is important also to understand that "we" are only able to experience what we are as I, for there is rigorously nothing else to be experienced. That "we" experience it as contrast between opposites, fundamentally positive and negative but affectively as pleasure and pain, etc., is an ineluctable effect of the duality of which "we" are constituted as concepts in "mind."

"We" are conditioned to imagine that these contrasting elements can exist independently the one of the other, but such a simple-minded notion is untenable, as every student of philosophy, however elementary, must know. Unfortunately religions, impregnated with such notions from early times, tend to perpetuate this absurdity, which is an added and unnecessary obstacle to clear understanding, and one so elementary that it should not be allowed to hinder the deconditioning which leaves open the way to clear apprehension of the truth concerning what we are.

When this inevitable concomitant of duality, called relativity, is understood it should no longer be difficult to apperceive that with the disappearance of temporality as an objective existence independent of the perceiving of it, and its recognition as an intrinsic element in that perceiving, that thus it is subjective, the perfect equanimity which is our natural condition intemporally must necessarily supervene and replace all the miseries due to our supposed bondage to temporality.

❧

Arya Deva regards Space and Time as inferences, sensorially imperceptible *(Catuh Satadam ix.5).* If an object existed it could not change—change being movement in duration, the illusion of "stills" or quanta seen successively in mind, existing only in mind—as Hui Neng pointed out in settling the argument about the movement of the wind or the flag.

15 ~ The Subjectivity of Time

THE MAHARSHI (Sri Ramana) said, "What is *eternal* is not recognised as such, owing to ignorance."* Ignorance of what is "eternal" is due to the concept of "time," and so ignorance of eternality is a definition of that concept, since the eternal and a time-concept are interdependent counterparts, i.e. intemporality and temporality.

He continued: "Ignorance (the concept of 'time') is the obstruction. Get rid of it and all will be well. This ignorance (the concept of 'time') *is identical with the 'I' thought.* Seek its source and it will vanish."

The "'I' thought" is entirely a temporal product, depending upon and exclusively appearing to exist subject to temporal extension (duration). If you apperceive what "time" *is,* it must simultaneously dis-appear *as an object in mind.* It is then revealed as the essential element in the constitution of an I-concept or conceptual "I," and the I-concept as an object in split-mind must go with it, for neither what "time" *is* nor what "I" *am* can have any objective quality whatever.**

An "I-concept" and the "time-concept" are inseparable, neither can appear to exist without the other: they are dual

---

* *Teachings,* p. 118.

** In case there should be any misapprehension: "What 'time' *is*" is what split-mind tries to conceive as "Intemporality," just as "What I *am*" is what split-mind tries to conceive as "I," which respectively are only cognisable in relativity objectivised as "time" and as "me."

aspects of what is erroneously conceived as objective, and are themselves believed to have objective existence as such. That assumed objective existence of what is a concept-of-sequence in mind is precisely the foundation of the notion of "bondage." *Seeking to dispose of one aspect without the other is a labour of Sisyphus,* for the one that is left will inevitably bring back its fellow on which it depends. As long as the concept of "time" as an objective existence, as a continuity independent of the continuous perceiver of it, is left untouched, that object must retain its subject—and its subject, the perceiver of it, is precisely the I-concept in question.

That is why the nature of "time" should be revealed. In the distant past an analysis of the nature of "time" was not in accordance with current modes of thought and of general knowledge, so that no tradition of it was handed down by the Masters, who certainly understood it since they refer to it obscurely but quite often, but this is not a valid reason for us to ignore it. For us it should be readily comprehensible, and its comprehension is urgent, the more so since it will hardly be denied that many of the ancient traditional approaches to the essential problem have lost much of their force through unending repetition and the auto-hypnosis that accompanies the repetition of all kinds of popular concepts.

If the I-concept can be disposed of for a moment, and the concept of duration remains, the latter will restore the former which is extended therein and which remains with it. This, indeed, is a familiar occurrence, but its mechanism is not recognised. On the other hand, if the concept of duration is seen as invalid, as not an objective existence to which "we" can be bound, but as an essential part of our appearance, extended therein, being our-extension, *its removal must necessarily carry with it all that is extended in it.* Then the supposed objective character of both lapses, and the process of objectification ceases, leaving "us" as what intemporally we are.

As long as we continue to regard "space-time" as objectively factual we are not merely "bound"—we are *trussed!*

Note: What is termed "an I-concept" is a symbol of the splitting of whole-mind into relative duality, which consists in conceiving "other-than-self" as a space-time entity, whereby its interdependent counterpart "self" becomes another. This dual, or divided, functioning of mind (just termed "mind" by the Maharshi) appears as the conceiver or functioning "I," *temporally extended as "duration."* Therefore the Maharshi states "The mind is only the thought 'I.'"

16 ~ The Timeless Way

THE ONLY way of escape from subjugation to the concept of "time" as an objective factuality, external to ourselves, is by identifying ourselves with it, re-becoming it, which is apperceiving that it is what we are, not objectively but subjectively.

When we recognise ourselves as temporality, we have only to apperceive what is obvious—which is that temporality and intemporality are inseparable, each being an aspect of the other, the one appearing in movement, the other static. They may be said to be twin modes of cognising what we are, temporality accompanying and making possible all phenomenal action, and intemporality remaining noumenally eternal.

As such the one may be said to be what we are as *prajña,* the other what we are as *Dhyana.* Noumenally we are intemporal, phenomenally we are "time," the one *nirvanic,* the other *samsaric.*

But they only have conceptual existence, and neither is as any "thing" in itself.

As "time" we are intemporal, and as "intemporality" we are time.

Of course as the one we appear to be singular, as the other to be plural, but our plurality is as conceptual as our singularity. We are neither—for what-we-are is not any "thing" that could have any conceptual quality or attribute whatsoever. It is neither any "thing" nor no "thing," for it is void of "thingness"—which is objective and conceptual only.

We can all say "Intemporal, I am Time: temporal, I am Eternal."

17 ~ Succession, Dialectically

IN ORDER to experience "duration" we must necessarily be what "duration" is, or "duration" must be an aspect of what we are, for "duration" is not some vague entity independent of the experience of it.

What we experience—we *are.* Conceptualising experiences, diversely named as opposing and mutually contradictory counterparts, emotions, sensations, etc. *cannot be anything apart from the cognising of them.* Their conceptual objectification as "other," as independent entities experienced by a "self," is an untenable relative supposition to which we have become conditioned.

Also, since we are "duration," we cannot have been "born" and we cannot "die," because duration as such, or other than as a concept in mind, cannot begin or cease to endure, *since duration cannot start or stop enduring,* for otherwise it could not be duration at all. A conceptual object in mind may be supposed to start and to stop objectively experiencing "duration," but non-objective duration as such cannot be "duration" unless it endures.

It follows that since "time" is an aspect of what we are, we are temporal, and we must be intemporal also: since we endure, we can never cease to endure and we can never have begun to endure, for "time" cannot begin to be "time" or cease to be "time." "Time," therefore, is eternity, and there cannot be any difference between temporality and intemporality. The supposed difference can only be conceptual and due to the concept of *succession* which creates the illusion of "lasting."

Therefore "appearance and disappearance," as concepts, "birth and death," "creation and dissolution," must be psychic effects of the concept of "succession."

Time is subjective, but it is conceptualised as an object to which "we" are apparently subservient, but which is only an image in mind. In that respect and also, it is what we are—for what-we-are is subjective and is conceptualised as an object in mind which is not I but "me."

In relative phenomenality "we" are conceptual objects subservient to conceptual succession which creates the illusion of "lasting" in temporality, but noumenally we are Intemporality, "eternal" in the sense of transcendent to any conceptual interpretation of the notion of duration. As such, however, we are no longer plural, nor are we singular either.

Temporality is not in fact—but only in appearance—different from intemporality: each is a conceptual interpretation, positive and negative respectively, of the phenomenon of the sequential extension of objects, of their duration as opposed to their possible lack of duration. They lose all meaning in their mutual negation, which leaves the eternality which is what, ultimately, we are.

Ultimately the non-difference of all pairs of opposites lies in the absence of an experiencer of them.

18 · Walking Backwards into the Future

I

DO WE not see it the wrong way round? We think we must do something, or not do something, so that a subsequent eventuality may, or may not, result.

But may not the contrary be what is required? Should not whatever we do, or refrain from doing, be in accordance with whatever eventuality is about to occur?

Is it not with what is in process of becoming apparent in the time-sequence of manifestation *that we should be in accord,* rather than be concerned about the gratuitous and imaginary effect of some action we may envisage in a "present" that will already be in the "past" by the time that its performance has been cognised?

Do we see the essential absurdity of this conditioned notion that our apparent action could effect what is evolving in future time, which apparent action itself will already be in our "past" when we have experienced and cognised it?

The future is awaiting us in the sequence of "time," like a house that is being built for us, or a repast that is being prepared. The idea that *we* are building our house or cooking our repast—*we* who have no idea how to build unbuilt houses or to cook anything unforeseeable—is surely an illusion, a reversal of seriality, based on false premises—the false premises of autarchy and the recompense-or-retribution of volitional ethics, all of which looking-in-the-wrong-direction constitutes the chains of our pseudo-bondage.

II

Should we not reverse this retroactive error, abandon retrospection, and live prospectively instead, adapting our psychology to what is ahead instead of gratuitously assuming that what is ahead depends upon what has already occurred? We appear to assume that the "past" influences the "future," even that the "future" is the effect of the "past" which we are conditioned to see as its cause, but surely the contrary is at least as plausible if not altogether more evident.

Theoretically, of course, the future is neither more nor less dependent on the past than the past is dependent on the future. They are not two, they are not separate or different in nature, and the "present" which we imagine as an essential and factual link between them as two entities, has no more veritable existence than the equator.

Does the captain of a ship travelling South imagine that his ship can bring its own weather into the Southern hemisphere, instead of preparing it for the weather which is in store for it when it crosses the "line"?

We seem to imagine that we "belong" to the past, because we remember it, and that the future is non-existent because our memory does not record it, but that somewhat primitive reasoning may have led to an unjustifiable conclusion. The past has "passed" and should be left behind in our apparent temporal transit: the future approaches and it is for that we should be prepared and to which we need to adapt. We think we "belong" to the past, but there is no valid reason to suppose that such is the case: we have had it; surely do we "belong" to the future: which is about to have us. Such surely is our phenomenal position?

III

Noumenally no such discrimination can be in question, for there is no distinction between "past" and "future," and neither is either present or absent, for they represent our extension in duration, the temporal aspect of our intemporality, and their phenomenal separation is based on spatial extension in temporal sequence, in which neither "past" nor "future" could have any causal function in regard to the other. Rather have they—in their apparent sequence—a mutual or reciprocal relation.

Therefore what we become is as much and as little an effect or result of what we have been, as what we have been, or think that we are, is an effect of what we are becoming or shall have become when that becoming is passed. Otherwise expressed, our conceptual existence is as much or as little dependent on what it has apparently been in the "past" as on what it is about apparently to become in the "future."

What we appear to be, composed of mutual conceptions, can have no factual past or future, i.e. other than conceptual—or psychic if you prefer the image—since duration is only a sequential appearance in mind; the sequence of our appearance could be regarded, theoretically at least, in either direction, and its evolution may seem to depend causally on either what has appeared or on what has not yet appeared. Growing older may appear to depend on our having been younger, or our having been younger may appear to depend on our being about to be older.

We find it difficult to envisage this? That is only because it is inhabitual, which also is why it should help to break down conditioned thinking which gives us the illusion of bondage.

If we lay a bet and win, or lose, was not the laying of the

bet as much due to our winning it, or losing it, as the winning or losing of it was due to its having been laid? Would the bet have been laid but for its winning or losing?

Why do all things eat and reproduce? In order that living things may live at all. Is not their living as much the reason for their eating and reproducing as the latter is for the former? Which comes first—the living, or the eating and reproducing, the acorn or the oak, the egg or the chicken, and which is the cause of the other? Causation is an illusion—as every notion based on "time" as something objectively existing must necessarily be.

But if we were to live as belonging to the "future" instead of as belonging to the "past"—should we not live more freely?

And if we were to live knowing that we "belong" to neither, but that, being that of which we ourselves conceptually are composed, they *belong to us,* should we not thereby find that there is no freedom to be "found"—since all that "freedom" could be is precisely this which we are?

IV

So much for "living."

And "dying"? Is the trouble due to regret for what we are leaving, or for what we shall not have in the future? To worry about what we are losing, or to worry about what may be coming?

Is dying to the past so tragic for us—or is it dying to the future which we shall not know? Would we care so much if it were only the former, of which we may have had enough?

Would we accept it more serenely if we saw it as only the latter? If so, we are now dying to the past, as we have lived to the past, rather than to the future.

But if we lived to the future, then our dying, as our living, should be more serene.

Then instead of "my past obliges me to do this, I am acting so that the future shall be as I wish or think it ought to be," we might say "The future *requires* that I shall do this, that I shall act in this manner in order that I may become what I must become and that everything may be as it is due to be."

Would not conflict have vanished, strife have disappeared? We might be humble and more resigned? For is not humility just absence of anyone to be proud, and is not relinquishment just absence of anyone to renounce?

Note: The notion that the future is the result of the past is itself the result of deeply-rooted conditioning. It may be seen as fundamental in our thought. As has been pointed out, it is based on the evident fact that "memory" is only retroactive. But this deep-rooted conviction need not be any the less unfounded for being deep-rooted. Deep rooted it is, and unfounded also, for it has no sound basis whatever. It is a temporal illusion, a deviation of the psyche, and it should rapidly disappear—along with others of its kind—if we were to break through the conditioning which binds us, and see clearly, without bias, our relationship with what we know as "time." That should be non-objective relation and, so-looking, we should find that our future no longer depends on our past, and our past can no longer be held responsible for our future.

The situation would not then in fact be "reversed," but such temporary "reversal" may be needed as a measure whereby a readjustment of our inaccurate perspective may occur, for this error in our direction of living in itself may be held responsible for our apparent condition of bondage.

An attempt to apply the foregoing analysis by means of isolated volitional actions would be unlikely to effect the psychological re-orientation which is here suggested.

19 ·⁓ So We Are Told

IN THE context of re-birth an aeon or a *kalpa* should be something like a minute of our duration called "time." Are we not re-born every *ksana,* 4,500 times every temporal minute, 270,000 times every temporal hour, 6,480,000 times every temporal day?

We can never be "enlightened" in the present "birth"—for we have no "time" to know it; nor in the next, nor in any other—for never have we "time" to experience it (or anything else). Perhaps that is why there is no such "thing," why there can be no "things" of any kind? It is what we are—unborn. Both born and unborn—and dead?

How can we be born? What we know as "life" is a thousand million births, and as many deaths. How can we die? What we know as "death" is a million deaths, and as many births. All that is clock-business, toys, gadgets and gimmicks—imagined stuff in an illusion of sequence.

"Meantime" (meaning "beyond time": that odd Buddhistic meaning of "mean") we are only what we are outside the notion of "time," unborn, undead, and so blazing with "light" that we are Enlightenment Itself?

Note: This is good Indian Buddhism. Tibetans claim to have trained themselves to perceive the *ksana,* which should correspond exactly to the "stills" whose rapid succession in projection on to a screen—our "mind"—produces the illusion of movement to the famous "Observer."

"A *ksana,* the shortest space of time, a moment, the 90th part of a thought, the 4,500th part of a minute, during which 90 people are born and as many die." In view of the two figures of 90, a *ksana* would appear to be what we are. Enough? Or already too much?

For those of us who insist on "being," at any price—is this not a tolerable hypothesis? Better than swallowing the literal notion hook, line, and sinker? It almost can be said to "work"?

20 ∙ The Great Pearl (Hui Hai) Concerning "Time"

> There is no single thing *(dharma)* which can be grasped or rejected. *When you cease looking on things in their temporal aspect,* as having come or gone, then in the whole universe there will be no grain of anything which is not your own treasure. . . . Do not search for the truth with your intellects. Do not search at all. The nature of mind is intrinsically whole. Therefore it is written in the Avatamsaka Sutra: "All things have no beginning, and all things have no end."

Note: "'Your own treasure,' *relatively* an objective concept of possession, here is used to imply something like "the *absolute* value of what you are."

In relative language his revelation could hardly be clearer. We have only to apperceive it *directly.*

Big Joke

As long as we go on tacitly accepting "time and space" as veritable, anything we say or do must necessarily be nonsense metaphysically, or, more politely, just fun-and-games.

We close our eyes to them presumably because we instinctively know that their inevitable invalidity blows the whole structure of phenomenality sky-high: for nothing but "noumenality" could survive.

21 · Intemporal Time

As "TIME" we are "intemporality," and as "intemporality" we are "time," for time and intemporality are not different in undivided mind.

Therefore our temporal aspect implies and requires our intemporality.

But we can also say that we are neither "time" nor "intemporality" for neither as such is anything but a concept in divided mind.

Conceptually, however, there can be no difference between "intemporality" and "total absence of time and of no-time"; the latter is a double negative abolishing no-time, i.e. that kind of time which is "no-time"; or negative time as well as positive time.

Time-less or time-full, we are still conceptually "time," for such, conceptually, we must necessarily be.

Positivity is temporal and finite,
Negativity is timeless and infinite,
But neither exists otherwise than conceptually.

22 · Quips and Queries - I

How could anything extended in the concepts of "space" and "time" be other than a fabrication in mind, as a dream is?

Existence is subject to Time. How could what-we-are be dependent on sequence in duration?

Can any metaphysical statement based on a tacit acceptance of space and time be anything but balderdash?

The seeker is the found, the found is the seeker—as soon as it is apperceived that *there is no time.*

All "being" can only "be" as a continuity in duration. That is why the Diamond Sutra condemns it as a concept which has no existence as such.

Phenomena are not extended in space-time objectively, as things in themselves: it is the perceiving which extends them.

"Sudden enlightenment" means precisely the immediate apperception of all that in fact we are.

"Enlightenment" is "sudden" only because it is not in "time" (subject to sequential duration). It is re-integration in intemporality.

Apart from the conceptual "space-time" of relativity in which it is extended—there is nothing for "form" to be.

PART II

Sentience

The Buddha forebore to specify: as long as there is any "one" to suffer—he will.

23 - Should Not This Be Said? . . .

Must not this be said? Can it be said with sufficient finality? How may it be stated with a force and conviction that leave no room for even a shadow of equivocation?

As long as an apparent individual thinks, as long as he is speaking, acting, or cognising, as an autonomous entity, self-identified as such psychically and somatically, can such a pyscho-somatic apparatus so-acting be qualified to understand what it is?

Can a psyche-soma, presuming its factual existence to be what is sensorially apparent and intellectually cognisable, be capable of knowing, and so of saying, anything significant or accurate concerning its fundamental nature?

Otherwise expressed, can anybody who is still thinking of himself as a "self," speaking and acting as such, be comprehending the essential error in consequence of which everything so being thought and said must of necessity be erroneous also?

More concisely, can anything of metaphysical import, that "anyone" says, thinking and speaking as, by, and from a supposedly autonomous entity, be anything but arrant nonsense?

This idea does not necessarily imply that only a fully disidentified sage can say anything pertinent; it means that anything pertinent can only be said by or via a psycho-somatic apparatus whose cognition is intuitional and immediate, based on impersonal perception, and on a clear understanding of the origin of what is then functioning.

So why "must this be said"? In order that the essential understanding may break through, and that we may know ourselves for what we are and for what we are not.

Note: Such a statement may be not only disagreeable to read, but is likely to hurt the feelings of sensitive and well-intentioned readers who believe they know a great deal about these matters, and who indeed may "know" a great deal, perhaps considerably more than the writer of these lines. But, if that be so, it is itself a valid reason for such a statement and, if it has not been made heretofore, the present writer must share the accusation of cowardice that may be presumed to be responsible.

General statements have indeed been made, such as "Everything we say must necessarily be untrue"—and everyone is delighted, almost flattered, but then everyone is involved and hardly anyone takes it seriously! Such a general assessment is even more profoundly true, but does it help anybody and does it serve any immediate purpose? in order to be effective truth must penetrate like an arrow—and that is liable to hurt.

❦

"*Objective* existence is only a notion,"
(And surely somewhat fatuous at that?)
Why so?
All "existing" is objective
And there is no one, and no "thing," to exist.
Is not this the whole, the sufficient, the ultimate truth?
Can we know any other?

24 ~ An Ego, A Self . . .

An ego, a self, or an individuality, can only be conceived as an object extended in space-time.

When time is recognised as a spatial measurement interpreted as sequential duration, i.e. as a series of "stills" or quanta perceived as movement, the purely conceptual nature of all possible objects becomes evident. Such is the composition and nature of all phenomena, and the sensorially perceived universe is nothing else.

As phenomenal objects we are only that, but if we were only phenomenal objects we could not know phenomena as such, for "the perceived cannot perceive," as Huang Po stated, i.e. if we were flowing in the stream of time we could not know it was flowing. What-we-are cannot be in the temporal stream in which objects appear to us, therefore we must be intemporal, outside the stream of sequential duration within which objects appear.

An autonomous "self" that "lives" and "dies" is necessarily a part of this temporal phantasy which is responsible for a see-er, thinker, actor, and things seen (or otherwise sensorially perceived), thoughts and deeds. There have never been any such entities otherwise than as *figurants* in the phantasy, but the function-ing implied—the doing as opposed to the do-er or the deed apparently done—is functional, that is not a conceptual interpretation of a percept but perceiving as such, which is the subjective or prajñatic aspect of immutable Dhyana or what we are.

That is why "think*ing* and feel*ing*" in their functional aspects, uninterpreted as thought and emotion, are not then subjected to the dualistic process of subject and object in a time-sequence of A thinking a thought, or B feeling an emotion; they are still impersonal, non-objective, and are not yet apparently experienced by an experiencer, but are the experience-ing which is all that in fact "he" can be.*

---

* In order to "experience," to suffer any "experience" relatively, we must necessarily be what we "experience," for what "experience" *is* must be what we are absolutely.

They can be described as "insee-ing" and "infeel-ing," as long as the "in" is not in reference to an implied see-er or experience-er looking "within," but to the "within" which is the source of the function-*ing*, which is what he is, that is not to any phenomenal object that might be supposed to be suffering experience but to the origin of all apparent manifestation including seeing and feeling. The terms should be less misleading as "within-seeing" and "within-feeling."

Such thought, called "the One Thought" by Shen Hui, or "a thought of the Absolute (absolute thought)," and such impersonal non-objective affectivity, is not an interpretation of quanta as movement, is not, therefore, temporal: it is the *arrière-fond*, the immutable background of the phenomenal process of "living." It is *Dhyana*, what-we-are, in our functioning aspect called *Prajña*. Subjected to sequential duration it becomes thought and emotion, concept and ratiocination, love/hate, and pleasure/pain.

The Goose

"Destroy 'the ego,' hound it, beat it, snub it, tell it where it gets off?" Great fun, no doubt, but where is it? Must you not find it first? Isn't there a word about catching your goose before you can cook it?

The great difficulty here is that there isn't one.

25 ⁓ Sentience

"Living" is experiencing in duration.
Objective "life" is subjection to experience.
But only the non-objective is what we are.

"Being sentient" is suffering "experience" and, being the object of experience, gives the idea of individuality, of being a "self." What-we-are does not experience, can not experience at all. For only an object can suffer experience.

Identification with *that* which is suffering experience is what constitutes bondage, whereas "being-*this*-experience," devoid of entity, cannot be bound.

To experience is *paskein*—to suffer, whether interpreted as positive or negative "suffering." The "abolition of suffering" is *nirvana,* awakening to what-we-are, and what-we-are cannot suffer, since—not being an object—there is no "thing" to suffer.

Suffering, therefore, is conceptual, i.e. "experiencing" in a time-context.

Phenomenally, that experience-ing (being sentient) is what, extended in space-time, we are, whereas we imagine that we are some "thing," an "individual" self that has, that possesses, a body and a soul that is sentient and suffers experience. Such a pseudo-entity is a medium for suffering experience, and we are not to be identified with the objective medium whereby we are experienced.

Therefore, phenomenally, this sentience, spatially extended in duration, is our "self-nature": only the "being," that is imagined as subjected to suffering, is illusory.

And this same "sentience," not extended in space-time, potential, devoid of objectivity, and not being experienced, not "suffered," is our noumenal identity, called the Absolute, Bhutatathata, Dharmakaya, Tao—or what you will.

Note: There does not seem to be, and can hardly be assumed to be, any justification for supposing that the Buddha, by appellation incarnate enlightenment, intended the word translated as "suffering"—whatever it may have been in the language he spoke, i.e.

Maghadi—in the negative sense only, that is as applying solely to that kind of experience which we regard as disagreeable. His vision was total vision, and "suffering" *(paskein)* means "experience"—whether cognised as "sorrowful" or "joyous."

The extent to which the Buddha's message may have been distorted by this sentimental and stultifying limitation, treating one element of a pair of interdependent counterparts as though it could have independent existence, has not yet—to my knowledge—been estimated. No doubt it could be maintained that Mahayana itself, particularly as represented by the Supreme Vehicle (Shresthyana), in fact represents a rectification of this somewhat ingenuous interpretation. It is clearly stated in the second section of Heart Sutra (see *Open Secret,* Part III, 42:I).

❧

Receptivity

Yung Chia said: "Ask a wooden puppet when it will attain Buddhahood by self-cultivation."

Was he referring to sentient-beings as "wooden puppets,"

Or was he implying that they could do what puppets cannot do?

Puppets can only react to stimuli. Sentient-beings can both react to stimuli and act directly, activated indirectly (via volition) and directly by *prajña,* which is their sentience—the one "false" action *(yu wei),* the other true *(wu wei).*

Receptivity is not reacting to stimuli, but lying open to *prajña,* which is *dhyana,* whole-mind, and what-we-are.

26 · Sunshine—A Dialogue

Hui Hai, on the first page of his treatise on Sudden Enlightenment, explains it by saying that it is a means of getting rid of conceptual thinking. An instantaneous means. But how?

He tells us that also; does he not add that "enlightenment" is just the apperception that "enlightenment" is not anything to be obtained, to be obtained or attained by anyone soever?

He does, but what does he mean?

If he had wished to answer that question would he not have done so? He wished us to answer it, to insee the answer. It should be seen directly, not indirectly via a Master, not intellectually as knowledge, but by whole-mind. It is for you to see it.

We are told that it means that it cannot be attained because we have it already, that it is always ours.

Typical half-baked nonsense! What are we, phenomena, to have or possess that or anything else? That is the usual pitiful attempt of volitional consciousness to maintain its position as an entity!

Then he means to imply that "enlightenment," "awakening," "liberation," or whatever term one uses, is not any "thing," that there isn't any such thing anywhere, or nowhere, to be obtained or attained?

No doubt that is a fact, but why? What conclusion do you draw from that?

If it is not there, we cannot have it!

That is not the point. What does the absence of an object connote?

The absence of a subject.

The absence if its subject!

You mean there is neither object nor subject, which are inseparable, that there is no one to do it, neither doer nor anything done?

Never mind what I mean; is it a fact?

Yes, it must be a fact.

So what?

There is no "us" to have or to do anything whatsoever!

Good! Is not that the point?

I suppose it is. But what, then, are "we"?

Did not Hui Hai start by telling, actually telling, you that?

He told us that "enlightenment" was a means of being rid of conceptual thinking.

Exactly.

You mean that "we" are "conceptual thinking"?

Can you suggest a better definition of what we imagine that we are?

I suppose not! So that "enlightenment" is ridding ourselves

of what we imagine that "we" are?

Yes, and "suddenly," once and for all "time."

But, then, who does it?

There is no "who." Nothing phenomenal, evidently, if anything is done.

But is anything done?

What could there be to "do"?

No do-er and no-thing done. So what?

Neither subject nor object, and out of "time."

Yet there is some—let us say adjustment, or integration.

Adjustment or re-*integration.*

Even that needs doing!

A doing that is no-doing, action that is non-action.

Taoist *wei wu wei?*

Yes, and that implies? . . .

It must be what-we-are!

Quite so. What else could it be?

So that is the whole story! Everything is therein! There is no "us" at all, never was and never will be!

Because there is no "time" in which to "last" and no space in which to be "extended," since both are just concepts in mind.

There is no "us" either to experience "enlightenment," to be awakened from a "sleep," or to be freed from any kind of "bondage"!

Go on! Why not add—and no enlightenment, no sleep, and no bondage either? And how so?

Because there could not be one without the others, nor any others without the one!

That is surely the "doctrine that is no-doctrine" of Bodhidharma, the "transmission outside the Scriptures," which is the definition of Ch'an, the burden of "Ekayana"—the Supreme Vehicle.

Written and read its significance is not apparent, but suddenly apperceived it is luminous—like the sun emerging from behind the clouds!

What we are is the sun; "we" do not dissipate the clouds in order to reach (obtain or attain to) it: it is the sun which dissipates the clouds and enlightens us without us even knowing that "we" are there?

"Enlightenment" does not exist phenomenally at all, and "we" cannot have it—because it is what-we-are!

27 ·- What Noumenally We Are . . .

I

WHAT NOUMENALLY we are, commonly called "Sentience," unaware of sentience, as such is necessarily insentient: what we are phenomenally, called "sentient," is awareness of being sentient.

Also what noumenally we are, called "Presence," unaware of being present, as such is phenomenally absent: what we are phenomenally, called "Present," is awareness of being present.

Unconscious Sentience and Presence, therefore, are the noumenality of our phenomenal being-sentient and being-present.

Unconscious Sentience, phenomenally absent, becomes conscious of sentience only in the process of objectifying what-it-is, as sentient phenomena.

Likewise, unconscious Presence, phenomenally absent, becomes conscious of presence only in the objectifying of what-it-is, as present phenomena. Only phenomena, objects, can be sentient and present.

II

Sentient and present phenomena, manifested, conceptually extended spatially and in apparent duration, can have no autonomy whatsoever. Their only being, apparent also, lies in their noumenal Sentience and noumenal Presence, both as such phenomenally absent. Their manifested appearance is entirely in "mind," in a conceptual universe, which itself is objectification devoid of factuality, as are all forms of psychic manifestation such as dreaming and what has been termed "hallucination."

Sentient and present phenomena, as what they are unmanifested, defined here in conceptual terms as Sentience and Presence (or "Consciousness" or "Awareness" or, Vedantically, as "Being"), unextended in conceptual space and duration, are total *phenomenal* potentiality. As integers they are not at all in any sense that can be conceptualised, but their noumenal potentiality is absolute and inclusive of all conceivable manifested expression, which is expression by means of, and subject to, the duality of an apparent conceiver and what is apparently conceived.

There can be no noumenal "existence" as such, for all forms of existence, and its absence, are the product of the dualistic mechanism of conceptuality, which is the objectivisation of the noumenal which as such has no phenomenal "existence" whatever.

❧

Phenomena ARE "mind,"
All that is sensorially-perceived IS "mind,"
And we are the perceiving sentience.

Sentience as such is phenomenal experience of "mind,"
And "mind" means, and is, noumenon.

The apparent existence of phenomena
Is the apparent existence of "mind,"
But we can only be conscious of "mind,"
When we become aware of noumenal presence.
Using the word "I" to indicate our phenomenal absence.

28 ~ *Let Us See*

I

HAVE YOU ever noticed how often the great Masters seemed unable to understand why their monks found it so difficult to apperceive, how often they said "but look! It is just here!"? Let us try and see the meaning of this.

The teaching of all the greater Masters is simply to enable us to understand that objectivisation is what hinders us from apperceiving what in fact we are. What is translated as "thinking" means conceptualising—fabricating objects in mind. As long as we do that we can only perceive "that": we cannot apperceive "This," and the apperceiving of "This" is just awakening from the dream of an objective universe to the actuality of what is.

But what-is is nothing objective and cannot be objectified in any way, which means that it cannot be conceptualised. That is not some obscure mystery, as is supposed, but an absolutely obvious and logical inevitability. As has so often been pointed out here, it is merely because what is looking cannot see "looking"; what is conceptualising, or functioning in any manner, cannot observe "functioning," and "it" cannot be observed because it is not any kind of object, being the subject of all objects. There is absolutely no mystery about it. All speculations end in the so-called "Void," but there is no such thing: it is what is not there. It is "here," if you like, metaphorically speaking, and, being "here," being the looking, it cannot be seen by itself. Of course "it" has no "self," but if you have to say that it is a "self," *phenomenally* inexistent, you are not far out. Phenomenally absent, absence as such, "it" is noumenally present, presence as such. Words, fundamentally dualistic and phenomenal, cannot take us nearer.

Most of the "methods" advocated comprise a cessation of "thinking," but it has been widely observed—and anybody can verify it—that this demands an effort that cannot be long sustained. The inference seems to be that if such effort could be sustained, conceptualisation should cease and what is termed "enlightenment" (awakening to what we are) would supervene. Few things could be more unlikely, however. What is operating here is positive, since it implies effort, and what is apparently functioning is a conceptual "I" desperately trying to pull itself up by its own boot-straps. Awakening to what we are requires no phenomenal effort: it just happens, and all "we" can do is to allow it to happen. Nor do we normally give it much opportunity. Why, because its opportunity is our absence as "I." The situation must be vacant. As long as "we" are conceptualising, the situation is not vacant, for trying not to conceptualise is a precise and potent form of conceptualisation.

There is not, cannot be, any prescriptive method of not conceptualising: it can just—lapse. And it is more liable to lapse when "we" have understood that conceptualising is not the only way of living and thing-we-can-do. Sitting down in a very uncomfortable position (for us), with our legs under our chin, and concentrating on not-thinking, or on some positive nonsense such as "love" of someone or something, can only affirm our conceptual "I." One might, perhaps, say: the conceptual absence of what is conceived HERE—is what I am; or, the present absence which is what I am, is the absent presence of my appearance.

This may read like a cosy little chat, but it need not be regarded as such. If that is all it is, I am doing it very badly—which is by no means unlikely. But it is improbable that writing bombastically makes it any easier. All I am trying to point out is that as long as we are conceptualising we are "out," and as soon as we cease to conceptualise we are "in." I suggest that it is as simple as that, and that people who say otherwise seem to be talking through their hats. The furthest we need go to meet them would be to say that the moment we cease our conditioned attitude of permanent and unremitting conceptualisation regarding all things whatsoever—we are comfortably seated in a *bodhimandala,* which is a metaphorical "gazebo" or shrine in which awakening to the obvious, the so very very obvious, may supervene at any moment.

In short, our whole trouble—if trouble it seems to us—is our conditioned notion that nothing can be that is not a concept. This, of course, also happens to be true; in fact nothing whatever we regard as existing is other than as a concept in mind. But what we are is not any thing, of that kind or of any other kind, and we can never reintegrate what we are by means of our habitual conceptualising. This habit is so ingrained that we cannot normally imagine anything that is not conceptual, and we endeavour to imagine what we are in the same way, which, as has been stated, is forever impossible.

The flaw in the argument of most people is the notion that our conditioning is too great to allow us to understand anything otherwise than as an object. I am not able to believe that it is so, and go so far as to suggest that it is quite easy and that anyone can do it at any moment. Unfortunately most writers refuse to give us a chance, whereas I am writing this just to say "try it and let it happen." Did not Jesus Himself remark "Knock, and it shall be opened unto you"? But there is knocking and knocking; if you knock hard the Porter may be annoyed; he may ask who is this egoistic individual, just the type we do not accept Here! In fact perhaps the "knock" is no more than an availability to enter, which is no entry—since we are already within without knowing where we are.

Have I said it even now? Objectivisation is the only obstacle, but it does not need a substitute: a counter-force of equal strength is not what is required: *we are what subsists when it is absent.*

II

It is externalising instead of internalising. The phenomenal universe is perceived "without" whereas it should be apperceived "within"—as every sage and prophet, including Jesus, has pointed out, wherein it becomes "the kingdom of Heaven."

The noumenal reason is equally radical: phenomena are extended in "space" and have duration in "time," without which they could not be perceived, and without which there could be no perceiver: both must "last" in order that any thing can be known at all. Such is the essential characteristic of phenomenality, whereas noumenality, having no characteristics whatever, knows no such limitations.

Concepts are extended in space-time, therefore, for they are phenomenal, and the concept of "not-conceiving" is maintained, for as long as it can be maintained, in the degree of "time" which clocks can measure. And it is maintained by an act of volition, which is the conceptual-I functioning; whereas only in the absence of a conceptual-I could it be possible for what-we-are to replace that concept.

Noumenality, quite evidently, cannot manifest itself directly in a time-context, since its manifestation as such is only possible subject to space-time, wherein it divides into apparent subject and object and operates via the mechanism of opposing interdependent counterparts—which operation results in the phenomenal universe. Space-time can only be phenomenal, noumenality knows it not, and nothing phenomenal can be directly noumenal for there is a solution of continuity between them. Noumenon is transcendent to phenomena, but it is immanent therein.

Thus every concept is subject to space-time, and every concept can only be true phenomenally, so that nothing "we" can say conceptually could possibly be true noumenally: what we call "truth" phenomenally, conceived by split-mind, must necessarily be nonsense noumenally to whole-mind. It then follows that neither conceptualising nor not-conceptualising, the positive and negative aspects of conceptuality, can open the way to noumenality. As long as "we" tacitly accept the factors of "space" and "time," themselves interdependent as "space-time," nothing we say or do can have noumenal validity. "Space-time" it is that constitutes the "insurmountable obstacle," and only in the absolute silence of the mind, which is conceptual absence, can "we" cease even for an instant to seem to be what-we-are-not in order to find integration in what-we-are.

Note: Saying it simply: there is no *phenomenal* way out.

29 ·– Happiness

Happiness is dependent on duration: it can only appear to exist in the sequence of "time." Moreover nobody can know that he is happy—an animal doesn't, a child doesn't; a man may know it afterwards. Therefore happiness can only be an effect of memory.

You look at an animal, a child, a man, and you say "he is happy"? It is you who see it: he doesn't. You may be right, but it is you who *recognise* whatever you mean by "happiness": what you recognise exists in you, and nowhere else wherever.

Moreover in you also it only appears to exist in relation to memory—memories of memories of something you never knew otherwise at all.

You say that you can train yourself to recognise it almost at once? Almost—but not quite, for even then it belongs to the "past." In order to know what it is you cannot any longer be subject to the passage of "time," which means that you can no longer be "you," and that "it" cannot any longer be "happiness"—for then, what it is—you must be.

It never existed at all: it is merely your interpretation from memory of your own intemporal nature.

I am: it is you who supply the details—and they are whatever your reactions may imagine, but they belong to "you" and not to "me"—for there is none such, other than in your mind.

Note: When a dog is released from a rabbit-trap in which his paw has been caught, he bounces with delight? When you win a bet at long odds, or receive any unexpected satisfaction, you also bounce with delight? Quite so. That proves, if proof were necessary, that all counterparts are mutually dependent, more spectacularly revealed in cases of sudden contrast, but experienced after all departures from a norm. However long or short its duration in a time sequence, it is always a memory that you "enjoy," never the event as it is occurring.

In myself I am nothing, exactly no thing: I am only a mirror in which others see aspects of themselves and attribute the resulting concepts to "me." But I am also an "other" to my "self."

30 · "Suffering" in Buddhism

WHEN THE Buddha found that he was Awake during that night under the bodhi-tree it may be assumed that he observed that what hitherto he had regarded as happiness, as compared with suffering, was such no longer. His only standard henceforward was *ananda* or what we try to think of as bliss. Suffering he saw as the negative form of happiness, happiness as the positive form of suffering, respectively the negative and positive aspects of experience. But relative to the noumenal state which now alone he knew, both could be described by some word in Maghadi, the language he spoke, which was subsequently translated as *dukkha*. *Dukkha* is the counterpart of *sukha* which implied "ease and well-being," and whatever the Maghadi word may have meant it remains evident that to the Buddha nothing phenomenal could appear to be *sukha* although in phenomenality it might so *appear* in contrast to *dukkha*.

This proposition is quite general and can be more readily perceived in the case of—say—humility. Humility is the negative form of pride, and pride the positive form of humility: they are not different as what they are but only in their interpretation. What we mean by true or perfect humility is not that at all: it is the absence of ego-entity to experience either pride or humility because, if humility is experienced, it rebecomes a form of its opposite—pride.

Similarly what we interpret as suffering and its opposite are just negative and positive experience, but when there is no longer a supposed ego-entity to experience either, neither can be present any longer, and what remains is *sat-chit-ananda* the division of which into three elements is merely a dualistic convenience. To require an accurate translation into Pali or Sanscrit of words in a lost language, long centuries before the dialectics of Nagarjuna, Arya Deva, and Candrakirti, is unreasonable, particularly in a tradition rooted in the Positive Way which is natural to Indians: it is the inevitable burden of the Buddha's teaching which concerns us rather than the dubious terms in which it may have been put into writing several centuries after his *parinirvana.*

31 · I Am but There Is No "Me"

I

WHAT IS called "experience" is the effect of reacting. It has no existence as such. It is sensually interpreted as pleasant or unpleasant, i.e. as positive or negative sensation, but it is conceptual, not factual.

What is it that *experiences?* Surely this is the ultimate question?

Must that not always appear as "me"?

Whenever there is experience, cognisance, is there not also the presence of "me"?

And vice-versa whenever there *seems to be* awareness of "me," must there not be a present experience?

Can either appear without the other?

Are they not—therefore—inseparable?

II

Experience, therefore, is inseparable from "me"; whenever it occurs a self, an object, experiences it. Always it is experienced by "me," never by "I" or by "you."

I cannot suffer experience, because only an object can appear to suffer, and I can never be anything objective—which is any thing at all.

Nor can "you" suffer experience, for in any kind of experience suffering is suffered *as "me"* and by "me," whoever seems to have the experience.

Therefore "experiencing" and "me" are both objects and

inseparable.

When I say "I suffer an experience," that is nonsense—for an experience can only appear to be suffered by an objective "me," and that experience and that "me" are inseparable.

This fallacious identification of what-I-am, of I, with "me," of subjectivity with objectivity, is precisely what is meant by "bondage": it is what "bondage" is.

For, *This I am,* but that "me" is not. A "me," like any and every object, is *sunya* and *k'ung,* existentially null and void, non-existent except as a concept in mind.

But since experience is a reaction to stimulus, the question subsists: what is it that reacts?

The answer is that what reacts is the experiencing of the experience, which is "me."

III

Therefore what is assumed to be the nominative "I" regarded as an object—absurd contradiction-in-terms as that is—referred to in the genitive, dative, and ablative cases as "me," and also in the accusative except when the verb that denotes "being" is used, is a sensorial apparatus whereby experience is suffered psycho-somatically.

It is indeed noteworthy that in the English language the concept of "being" should be reserved for "I." One may even be tempted to surmise that this abnormality might represent a deep-seated apprehension of the truth. Such phrases as "I am I," "You are I," "He, she or it is I," "We are I," are pure metaphysical expressions of the truth in so far as that could ever be stated in dualist terms. This is surely a sacred linguistic tradition if anything could be so-called!

The conclusion, both linguistically and metaphysically, is that I experience as "me."

From this it should follow that I, objectified as "me," as manifold "me," am experiencing as such, and that experience is the objective functioning of what I am.

Experience is reagent, it is an interpretation of a sensorial reaction to stimulus, but however complex or simple this mechanism in a context of space and duration may appear to be, it may be apprehended as the essential manifestation of what-I-am objectified as "me."

IV

May we not conclude, therefore, that since every sentient being appears to live and to experience, each one as "me," "living" as such is experiencing as "me," and every sentient being must therefore be an example of the objectification of I-subject, utterly in-existent phenomenally as such, but all that whatever is manifest can be assumed ultimately to be?

Since, however, nothing but what is phenomenal, which is objective, can be assumed to be—for neither the word "being" nor "existing" can imply anything but what is cognisable—we reach the inevitable conclusion that manifestation is not the manifestation of any objective "thing," which could only be a concept in split-mind. It must be mind as such, not in its divided aspect which produces phenomenality via subject-and-object, but its in-temporal and in-finite wholeness which can only be indicated by "I." Any sentient being, whose sentience it is, may say it, but none can ever know it, for wholeness could never be known since knowledge results from its division, and an object cannot know the subject which is all that it is.

I can know that I am it, for all I am is what it is, but what "it" is I can never know—for "it" cannot be any "thing" that could be known—otherwise than conceptually as each and all of "its" dualised phantomatic representatives objectivised as "you."

❦

To say "I" suffer is non-sense, for *I* cannot possibly suffer, since I have no objective quality that could experience any sensation whatever. But suffering, positive or negative, joy or sorrow, can be experienced by an identified "you" called "me."

32 ·- I, Noumenon, Speaking

I only am as all beings,
I only exist as all appearances.
I am only experienced as all sentience,
I am only cognised as all knowing.
Only visible as all that is seen,
Every concept is a concept of what I am.
All that seems to be is my being,
For what I am is not any thing.

Being whatever is phenomenal,
Whatever can be conceived as appearing,
I who am conceiving cannot be conceived,
Since only I conceive,
How could I conceive what is conceiving?
What I am is what I conceive;
Is that not enough for me to be?

When could I have been born,
I who am the conceiver of time itself?

Where could I live,
I who conceive the space wherein all things extend?
How could I die,
I who conceive the birth, life, and death of all things,
I who, conceiving, cannot be conceived?

I am being, unaware of being,
But my being is all being,
I neither think nor feel nor do,
But your thinking, feeling, doing, is mine only.
I am life, but it is my objects that live,
For your living is my living.
Transcending all appearance,
I am immanent therein,
For all that is—I am,
And I am no thing.

33 ·- The Positive Way

VEDANTA

Being-Aware may be said to be what noumenally I am.
All aspects of being aware are what phenomenally I am,
But these are devoid of being in themselves,
For they are manifestations of being-aware.

If awareness can be said to be cognisable at all,
Such cognising is ultimate inseeing,
And might be called "radiant voidness," manifesting as "Grace."
If I am aware of radiance—that may be awareness of what I am,

For, being Awareness, I am Radiance also.

What awareness is—I am,
What awareness seems to be—I am not,
Yet I am what every object is,
For every object is I.

The Negative Way

CH'AN

What I am must necessarily seem to be Unawareness,
Unaware of being aware.
It has been objectivised as "Voidness."

That is why I perceive awareness as my object,
Which I do not recognise as being what I am.
It has been objectivised as "Cognition."

This functioning, which is known as "cognising,"
Inevitably manifests in a conceptual extension,
Which is termed "space-time,"
And this is experienced by me as "living."

Since I can never become aware of my unawareness,
I can never be an object,
And I alone, of which I cannot be aware, cannot be known.

But everything of which I am aware,
Must necessarily be my object,
And therefore must be what I am,
For my object and I are not two.

34 ·– I: Why Are We Unaware of Awareness?

THE ANSWER is that split-mind, cognising by means of a subject cognising objects, cannot cognise its own "wholeness" as its object.

There is no need to cognise our "wholeness," and it is forever impossible to do so, for there is no "thing" here to cognise and no "thing" there to be cognised.

Any attempt to cognise what is cognising—and is thereby incognisable—forbids apperception of what-we-are. Such apperception is not a function of split-mind. It can only be an im-mediate apperception released by some sensorial stimulus—auditory, visual, tactile, or of an unrecognisable origin.

The supreme obstacle to such apperception, in our space-time context of consciousness, lies in attributing subjectivity to phenomenal objects, and objectivity to what is subjective.

Mind cannot be reached by mind, as Huang Po stated. The attempt is itself an obstacle. Awareness is no thing of which we (who are This) can be aware.

Knowing this, understanding this, is not awareness of Awareness. Awareness is no kind of knowledge. All knowledge is conceptual, all conceptuality inheres in the space-time continuum. There is a solution of continuity between knowledge and Awareness.

If one were to say that auditory apprehension might reveal it—such might be an indication of what is implied, but quite certainly not in the sense of deliberately listening to music—nor of deliberately looking at any object, touching any "thing," or seizing any thought.

Why is that so? Because split-mind must be in abeyance, and "we" must be absent for Awareness to be present.

II: In the Silence of the Mind I Sing

There is nobody and nothing to be aware of Awareness,
Awareness, I cannot be aware of myself,
For I know no self of which I could be aware.

I am no thing of which to be aware,
As a thing "you" cannot know awareness,
For "you" can only be aware as "I,"
When there is no "me" of which to be aware.

Divided into cognising subject cognising objects,
I cognise all that can be cognised,
Every conceptual thing save what is cognising,
Which, as such, is not conceivable, since it is no thing,
And is no thing, since it is not conceivable.

This is all I am, so simple am I,
Devoid of mystery, majesty, divinity,
Of any attribute whatever.
Being no thing,
How could I have the attribute of any thing?

Why try to glorify me?
I am neither glorious nor not-glorious,
I am neither anything nor nothing,
Neither the presence nor the absence of any thing.
I am this total phenomenal absence
Which is all that phenomenal presence can be.

Then how can I be known?
I cannot.
How can I be experienced?

I cannot.
Only "God" can be experienced,
And He is my concept, my object.

But when conceptualising is in abeyance,
Time is in abeyance also,
And space, together with all concepts.
Then all that you are I am.
You are my "self." I can have no other.

35 -- Definition of Prajña

I am the Hearing of hearing,
I am the source of all hearing, therefore I hear no sound,
I am the Seeing of seeing,
I am the source of all seeing, therefore I see no form,
I am the Feeling of feeling,
I am the source of all feeling, therefore I feel no touch,
I am the Smelling of smelling,
I am the source of all smelling, therefore I smell no odour,
I am the Tasting of tasting,
I am the source of all tasting, therefore I taste no flavour,
I am the Cognising of cognising,
I am the source of all cognising, therefore I know no concept.
Being the source of all sentience, I am Insentient,

Sound, sight, contact, odour, flavour, knowledge are not as such,
For what I am they are.

What is heard is my Hearing, seen is my Seeing, felt is my
Touching,
What is tasted is my Tasting, cognised is my Cognising,
But I am neither cogniser nor cognised,
For the suchness of cognising is my nature.
I am the Acting of acting, the Functioning of functioning,
But I neither act nor function,
I am the Experiencing of experiencing,
But I cannot experience experiencing,
For I have no self.
I am time-less and in-finite,
For what space-time is I am.

Note: As far as I happen to be aware, no one has stated in print what was factually implied by the terms *Prajña* and *Dhyana* as used by the great Masters of China—except Dr. Suzuki. Since this essential meaning is completely obscured by the usual scholastic rendering, the above attempted definition may be submitted.

Dhyana, of course, implies the static or potential aspect of what we are, whose dynamic aspect is *Prajña,* and *Prajña* may be described as the immanence of *Dhyana* which is our transcendence.

36 ·- Integrity of Mind—A Trilogy

I. IT ALL HAPPENS IN MIND
II. WHY SENTIENCE IS THE GATEWAY TO INTEGRITY
III. THE HEARING WAY

I. It All Happens in Mind

I

THE ENTIRE phenomenal universe is an appearance in what is termed "Mind," and this so-called "Mind" in which "we" all mutually appear, which objectively we perceive and cognise as the phenomenal universe, is what we all are—and all that we are.

II

This does not imply that this here-mind, this now-mind is any "thing" in itself, for quite certainly it is not, and to make an image of it as "Mind" in mind is merely to make an image of what is making that image—which could only render its apprehension forever inapprehensible.

But if this is understood perhaps the way lies open for cognition, though neither that term nor any other can even suggest what is implied, since every term is relative to its opposite. If there were two factors involved it might be done, but there are no two factors, nor one. Since we are not different or separate from "mind" we cannot "prehend" it, nor can we be "integrated" in it since we have never been disintegrated from it, and as long as we think in relative terms we can never understand what it is.

Nor can we know it by any means, for we are it, and our conceptual extension in what we call "space" and "time" gives us this illusion of duality whereby we are prevented not just from knowing what we are but rather from being it without having the absurd illusion that we *could* be anything *else*. We cannot "insee" it either, for there is no thing to insee or to outsee, no where to see in or out of, nor any one to do either.

What, then, is there to be done? When we are what we are do we need to be told what it is, to have it named or described? And could we understand it if it were? If there were only one man in the world—would he know he was a "man"? Would he be interested to know it? Does light know that it is "light"?

Is not that perhaps what the Masters meant by their obscure answer to the question of curious disciples enquiring how they knew when they were "enlightened"? They used an odd formula: they replied "When you drink water do you know whether it is warm or cold?" It was no answer, however varied or translated. But then the question was no question—and so could have no answer.

For split-mind cannot know mind that is whole.

All is this mind that we are.
If we could know this
What more could there be to be known?

II. Why Sentience Is the Gateway to Integrity

What is termed "bodhi" is the noumenal source of both "hearing" and "heard," of phenomenal sound and the hearing of sound, of the auditory object and of the subjective means of its being sensorially perceived.

The hearing-mind, like the seeing-mind, feeling-mind, knowing-mind, every apparently different aspect of sensorial mind is "bodhi." As such, all aspects of mind are subjective.

"Sound" is the hearing of sound. "Hearing" is the source of hearing. All sensorial perceiving is an expression of our nature as "bodhi."

The reception of all sense-perceptions is passive, but their source is active. Phenomenally objective, noumenally they are subjective—and their nature is called "bodhi."

But the nature of all objects is their subjectivity, since as objects they are only appearance, much as the only nature of shadows is their substance.

The subjective nature of all sense-perceptions, therefore, is "bodhi," which is our nature as phenomenal "perceivers."

As "bodhi" I am the light that cannot know darkness (or

light), the singing that cannot know silence (or sound).

We can say that every imaginable sound may seem to have been made, but no sound has ever been heard.

Why is that? What could there be to make a "sound"? Who could there be to hear one?

III. The Hearing Way

I

"Sound" has no meaning apart from the hearing of it, just as knowledge has no meaning apart from the knowing of it.

And the hearing of sound, like the knowing of knowledge, is sensory perception—objectively "sound" and "knowledge," subjectively the source of hearing, of knowing, and of all sensory perception, sometimes termed "bodhi," which inevitably is a name indicating what subjectively we are.

Thus every sound, and all forms of sense-perception, can lead us directly back to our source, as every *shadow to its substance,* which is the immutable wholeness of mind.

Other than "mind" there cannot be anything—for what else could there be, since nothing is cognisable otherwise than by mind? Mind alone cognises, and all cognition takes place in mind, yet mind "itself" is uncognisable since there is nothing to cognise it but mind and "it" cannot cognise the cognising which is all that it is.

"Mind," therefore, mind that is integral, itself is no "thing"—for a "thing" is only that which is cognisable, and mind could never cognise its cognising. The term "mind"—"noumenon" or "noumenality" in more technical language—is no more than an attempted definition of the present participle of the verb "to be," another of which is "I."

The Buddha is recorded as having stated, regarding the six

sense-perceptions, that while by their misuse they are the chief hindrance to our recognition of integrality (or whole-mind), they are at the same time our most direct means whereby such recognition of integrality may be recovered. He also stated that whereas all six senses are of equal value in these respects and that the apprehension of what any one of the six is reveals what all are, one—that of hearing—may be more suitable for a given phenomenal individual, such as Ananda, and could be regarded as being more direct. In saying this the Buddha confirmed and explained this same contention which had been so vigorously affirmed by both Avalokiteshvara and Manjusri.

What can be the rational explanation of this apparent anomaly? It can only be suggested that, particularly in bygone times, hearing was more important as a means of developing understanding than was seeing the written word, then relatively rare and available only to the learned. Not only was the spoken word more available but with the aid of metrical quality, by singing and chanting and the sound-manipulation of *mantra,* objective "sound" could lead back directly to our "hearing-nature," which is its subjective aspect, the substance of the shadow, which, like the nature of each other sense-perception, is what is called "bodhi." *Bodhi,* of course, is a term for our "enlightened" nature or the wholeness of divided and relative mind, which integrality is what we are, and which can only be indicated by the one unobjectifiable word in any language—which is "I."

Whether today the auditory "way" is any more direct or efficacious than the visual, the tactile, gustatory, olfactory, or cognitional "ways," may be a subject for discussion, also to what extent such efficacity may depend upon the propensity of a given self-constituted individual, but it may be doubted whether proficiency in the art associated with each "way" need necessarily be an indication of the suitability of that sensorial medium rather than an indication that it is not suitable. If a guess should be of any interest to anyone it might be that the disadvantages of experience and addiction might be found to exceed their advantages in this connection.

The efficacy of so-using any one of the senses which, if successful immediately releases the *mainmise* of all the others, assuredly does not depend upon skill, but chiefly upon understanding. It appears to be necessary that the process itself shall be in-seen and fully apprehended, indeed profoundly understood.

II

"Sound," therefore, is a phenomenal manifestation, an objectivisation in mind—for only in mind can it be cognised as "sound"—whose subjective element is "hearing," the hearing aspect of our sensorial-nature whose other aspects are "seeing," "feeling," "knowing," etc. But recognising "hearing" as our *hearing-nature,* the returning of "hearing" to its source, is merely re-objectifiying it as another concept in mind, whereas it is this "mind" which is responsible for the cognition, not the cognition as such, which is the reintegrating factor whose im-mediate apperception releases all the other aspects of sensory perception. But if "sound" can carry divided-mind that perceives it objectively *directly* back to its *wholeness,* this integrality thereby embraces all six apparently different sensory aspects of the split-mind which so conceives them, and nothing objective in them can remain.

What then obtains? Deprived of sensory objectivisation mind remains integral, and "otherness" can no longer be perceived as such. Differently expressed, if the apparently personal is seen as "other," all that was "other," including that personal "other," is seen as not-different from the so-seeing "self." Why is that? Otherness cannot be other than what is so-seeing, and where there is no "other" there can be no "self," where there is no "self" there can be no "other," and the absence of both is what I am.*

As a result, no phenomena is any longer an apparent objective *entity,* and all "things," absolutely all manifestation as such, are nothing but what is cognising.

In this process, inevitably instantaneous, both temporal and spatial extension lose their validity, i.e. they only retain their conceptual appearance in mind, as such, and no longer as objective reality.

This must inevitably be release from conflict, for nothing is any longer other than what it *is,* what necessarily it must be—since it is not other than its cognising.

So apperceived, all appearance is "in mind," apart from which nothing can appear, and "mind" is only a conceptual symbol for what is cognising and as such has no objective quality to be cognised.

---

* It is necessary that the objectivised phenomenon, hitherto mistaken for "self," be re-cognised as what it is in order that its non-objective relation with its subject way be established.

This concept also must be carried back to its conceptual source with the aspects of sensorial-mind of which it is composed, in order that integration may be complete. Total integration is equivalent conceptually to the total elimination of the objective (and so of the subjective) from cognising—and apart from cognising no experience could seem to occur.

Question: When you are looking at something does the thing looked-at exist objectively within the sphere of perception or not?

Answer: No, it does not.

Hui Hai, p. 48

37 · Returning Sentience to Its Source

Cease listening to what is being heard,
Listen to what is hearing instead!
Then listening will become what is hearing,
And hearing will be what is heard.

Cease looking at what is being seen,
Look at what is seeing instead!
Then looking will become what is seeing,
And seeing will be what is seen.

Cease seeking the sought of the seeker,
Seek what is seeking instead!
Then seeking will become what is searching,
And searching will be what is sought.

Cease cognising what is objective,
Turn sentience back on itself!
Cognising will become what is cognising,
And perceiving will be the perceived.

Leave sound unheard,
And "hearing" hear instead,
For hearing lives,
But sound, as such, is dead.

38 ~ *The Meaning of Mantra*

IT IS the conceptual content of the spoken word that distinguishes "speech" from "sound."

Speech as such could never "return" sound to "hearing." For such "return" only a meaningless word could suffice. That, no doubt, is the explanation of *mantra,* the "meaning" of which is not only inessential but intentionally obscure.

The *prajñaparamita* mantram in the Hrdya Sutra is thus explicable as what it purports to be, i.e. the supreme and most direct vehicle of awakening. No doubt this applies also to *Om Mani Padma Hum,* and all the others.

But let us not confuse the presence or absence of conceptuality in the words of the *mantram,* and the understanding that we are "returning" sound to hearing. Without that understanding neither a sonata nor the braying of a donkey should be likely to reveal the prajñatic factor: that understanding is fundamental in the sense of being the basis of the "event," and the "hearing," "seeing," or other sensorial perception, is merely the medium.

We should not overlook the fact that the "event" itself is phenomenal, a space-time performance, whereas the understanding, conceptually relative, non-conceptually does not appertain to split-mind but to its wholeness.

39 · The Meaning of Prajñaparamita

"Crossing over to the 'opposite shore'" implies turning from objectivisation to what may be termed "subjectivisation," which is "returning" the six senses to their source. This constitutes a "turning over of the mind" from externalisation to internality, from objectifying the "kingdom of the Earth" *without* to integrating the "kingdom of Heaven" *within*.

In this process each of the six senses should be turned back to their common denominator, but when any one such is so reversed they are all thereby, for their diversity is only apparent. To this reversion the terms *paravritti* and *metanoesis* also seem to be applicable.

This is a reversion from durational thought and sensation to im-mediate apperceiving unextended in "space" and "time."

Note: The traditional representation of this process, which is the mechanism of what is called "enlightenment," "awakening," etc., more accurately awakening to the enlightened state, as a crossing over of what-we-are to an objective "shore" which must then be what-we-are-not, is a catastrophic concession to our conditioned inability to think otherwise than by objectivisation. It is catastrophic because in itself it directly contradicts what we are being instructed to do in the statement itself, which thereby is rendered nonsensical.

The "crossing over" must necessarily be a metaphorical integration and could not be a disintegration, for the latter could only imply that what-we-are is phenomenal and that what-we-are-not is noumenal. Every concept based on our factuality as phenomena must necessarily be a turning-away from the essential understanding which is that phenomenality is nothing in itself, and that "bondage" is precisely and only that misapprehension. Release, by whatever high-sounding name it may be given, can only be an abandonment of that false identification, which thereby leaves us not re-identified but just dis-identified, and thus inconceivable by what is conceiving, which can only be represented by the *impersonal* pronoun "I."

40 ·- "Enlightenment," Relatively Considered

> There is a difference between Awakening and Deliverance: the former is sudden, thereafter deliverance is gradual. . . . In fact what we mean by 'Sudden Enlightenment' is the perfect equivalence of phenomenal understanding with universal principal: this is not reached by any stages at all.
>
> SHEN HUI

Has any Master left us a clearer statement? The sudden coincidence of relative comprehension with absolute apprehension, whereby the division of mind into subject and object is healed so that its wholeness supervenes, in a spontaneous absence of duration, throws open the way to deliverance from "bondage" to our conceptual universe.

With such authority, so simply stated, what "mystery" could remain, what could there be about which to argue?

We may continue to argue about the requisite preceding conditions, but the inescapable inference seems to be that relative perceiving and comprehending must lie open to absolute apperceiving and apprehending, for without the spontaneous im-mediacy of the apperceiving, the apprehension of unicity could hardly be assumed to supervene.

Temporality could never know intemporality, the divided know its wholeness, succession know eternality, and the totality of the Absolute cannot be supposed to cognise its temporal division. Only the sudden intervention of timelessness, an im-mediate and instant arresting of succession in duration, could be assumed to lay open the possibility of such integration, and no process or action subject to temporal succession could be supposed to produce such suspension of its own functioning.

Unicity is necessarily in-temporal and in-finite, and no temporal or finite interference should be either necessary or possible: it must supervene ineluctably at whatever moment in temporal and spatial extension a solution of successional continuity is presented.

Nor could such solution of continuity ever be volitionally produced in a context of duration: it could only occur as a temporal result of the maturity of the apperceiving and apprehending faculty which is inherent in all relative and sentient "beings" in order that they may be such. This faculty may be assumed to develop, in a context of duration, according to its potentiality, whereby apperceiving that I am no "thing" finds equivalence with apperceiving that I am all things, and integration supervenes.

It has often been said, but perhaps never so simply and with such perfect adequacy:

"Enlightenment, instead of altering our state, discloses what we have always been."

John Blofeld, *Hui Hai,* note 80

41 ∙ Gone with the Wind . . .

I manifest as Sentience.
In order to do so I extend conceptually,
Producing the appearance of "space" and "duration."

In order that I may be experienced
In this my space-time universe
I appear divided, so extended, as subject and object,
In order that, Subject, I may experience as object.

Thus "sentience" is not some "thing"
Experienced by an entity,
For when My conceptual subject and object are mutually negated
What remains is "I."

Manifested, subject-object discriminates sentience dually,
By opposing interdependent counterparts,
As "good and bad," "pleasant and unpleasant," "joy and sorrow."

But sentience is what subject-object is,
Because Sentience is what subject-object is as "I."

Note: Does this explain why what we "suffer" as experience is not some thing external to our "selves," suffered by a "me," but on the contrary is what we who are suffering experience?

Then—can suffering "suffer" suffering? Gone with the wind!

42 ·- *Quips and Queries - II*

Liberation

What is the use of trying to climb out of a hole we have never been in?

❧

I do not possess sentience:
What sentience is—I am.

❧

When the shadow of the ultimate object shall have disappeared, and nothing sensorially perceptible can be found, what then remains is what I am.

❧

"I do not experience distinctions like 'you,' 'me,' and so forth. Waking experiences are no more real than dream experiences." (Vasistha)

❧

WHAT *COULD* WE EXPERIENCE BUT WHAT WE ARE?
Experience should be communion.

❧

Ultimately the non-difference of all pairs of opposites lies in the absence of any one to experience them.

❧

We should never forget:
What we are looking for is what is looking.

❧

There is no OTHER which I can either like or dislike.

❧

What is called "Humility" is in fact just negative Pride, and is better so called, for the sole implication of true Humility is the absence of any entity to be proud.

PART III

The Conceptual Universe - 1

Only I-concepts quarrel,
For whoever knows what "he" is
There can be no "other"
Either to "love" or to "hate."

43 ~ *The Wrong Road*

PEOPLE IMAGINE that they must transform *themselves,* perfect themselves, become something else called a saint or a sage.

This is surely a great error and even greater nonsense. What is so thinking, is "himself" only a phenomenon in a dream or a character in a drama, or a manifestation subject to conditioning called "karma."

These must carry on their dreamed part, play out their role in the drama, suffer their "karma," in the seriality of "time" to the end. The "ego" they think that they wish to destroy, and which torments them and holds them in imaginary "bondage," is an inevitable and necessary part of their dream personality, of their "part," of their "karma," and they could not appear to exist without it.

Its disappearance is a degree of de-phenomenalisation and is a result of awakening from the dream, never a means thereto. The means thereto is just understanding what they are, that what they are is not the appearance, dream-personage, role, karma-bound puppet.

How could they "awaken" from the dream by "perfecting" their pseudo-selves which are being dreamed, etc., or otherwise than by re-cognising their veritable "identity" as the source of the dream, the drama, the phenomenal manifestation?

Note: An "I" is only a concept which assumes all the impulses which appear in the guise of "me"s.

Whoever thinks as from, or on behalf of, an entity which he believes himself to be, the more so if he tries to work on himself, by, with, or for such an entity—which is only a concept in mind—has not yet begun to understand what it is all about.

44 ·– Re-solution

MAY IT not, perhaps, be misleading continually and almost exclusively to stress the emptiness of apparent objects and the illusory character of the conceptual universe?

It is equally true to say that there is nothing *but* the conceptual universe, and there is not any thing outside it.

The source of its appearance is not apparent for there is no "thing" to conceive its source in order to render it apparent. And that is because all that appears is appearance and there can be no other appearance than what appears.

"We" are looking at it, perceiving it with our five senses and conceiving it with our sixth, and it is what "we" are that "we" are thus conceiving as appearance, for there is nothing else whatever at any time but what "we" are, nor anything but what "we" are that "we" could ever experience.

That also is why *there cannot be* such a thing as existence since there cannot be such a thing as non-existence, and vice versa, for there is no thing to be present or absent, since what appears is an image in mind.

That, too, is why there cannot be an entity, since there cannot be a non-entity, and vice versa, so that all appearance can only be described as such-as-it-is or "Suchness"—which term also denotes its origin.

Thus every sentient being is the source of the apparent universe *by means of his experiencing it as what he is,* for his "objectivity" is only an appearance in mind, and his "subjectivity" is the source of all experience.*

---

* Here the relative (philosophical) sense of "subjectivity," denoting the conative (volitional) posturing of an I-concept, evidently is not in question.

For true-perceiving is absolute functioning in this-here-nowness, and the apparent universe is this; so that the fundamental nature of all phenomena is the perceiving of phenomena.

Herein positive and negative vision approach integration, and the superficially contradictory statements of the Sages find their re-solution in Whole-mind.

Note: This should explain the famous three degrees of understanding, a rational elucidation of which is not vouchsafed: (1) mountains and rivers are perceived as such, (2) mountains and rivers are no longer perceived as such, (3) mountains and rivers are once more perceived as mountains and rivers—which is as sages perceive them.

&

The "question" of existence or non-existence is not a question, and is quite simple.

Phenomenally—for instance, as science sees it—only that which is objective can be said or known to exist.

Noumenally—as metaphysics sees it—since every object is appearance in mind—nothing objective can be said or supposed to exist.

Since subjectivity has no demonstrable existence, having no objective quality, it cannot be said to exist.

In short—objectivity and existence can be said to coincide.

45 - The Basic Invalidity of Science

IS SCIENCE valid? Either the world, and the entire universe, is as real as the word "real" itself asserts, or it is phenomenal (appearance) only, and appears to exist conceptually (in mind).

There is, therefore, a solution of continuity between the findings of empirical science and those of dialectic metaphysics. The former is entirely dependent on the phenomenon of sense-perception, the limitations of which are known and obvious, demonstrable in experimental science itself, and variable in kind, character and efficiency among different species of sentient beings.

Sensorially-based *knowledge* of a universe has thereby become a colossal structure of conceptuality, overwhelmingly convincing despite continual reversals of theory, to those who can accept the validity of what sense-perceptions report. But the validity of sense-perceptions as accurate records of realities objectively existing in their own right is, and remains, philosophically untenable. Moreover the whole conceptual edifice is extended in a spatial concept, on the validity of which it entirely depends, and also on sequential, or repetitive, duration in a time-concept whose "real"-ness as opposed to its phenomenality, is necessary to the initial existence of such a scientific universe—for by means of these that universe is perceived and measured and the relation of its parts is ascertained.

The metaphysical development of philosophy, however, not only questions but categorically denies, and dialectically disproves, the validity of concepts as possessing objective reality. The *Madhyamika* of *Nagarjuna, Candrakirti,* etc. may be cited as an example. So that thereby the ground is cut from under the feet of experimental science, and its vast structure is exposed as a colossal fabrication of mind, devoid of existence in its own right, the deduced "laws" of which are based on invalid assumptions according to its own system of logic, as well as upon intuitive apperception.

To an open mind the question thus posed must be: does the metaphysical extension of philosophy provide an alternative explanation of the apparent universe as sensorially perceived, and as interpreted and measured collectively, individually, rationally or instinctively, by different categories of sentient beings, from human to insectival? If it does not, then the claim may be justifiable that scientific methods are our only hope of understanding our relation to the phenomenal universe, and of knowing what that universe is. But if, on the contrary, it does satisfactorily explain what these are and their relation—which is the essential factor—and if we can clearly see that what it reveals must indeed be true—then the structure of Science stands revealed as a purely conceptual creation of the dualistic mind of man, with no validity that is not relative to spatial and temporal concepts.

Science, recognised as a conceptual structure, built on the shifting sands of sense-perception, can only exist in a framework of theoretical space-time, the assumed reality of which it makes no effort either to justify or to explain. As a conceptual interpretation of phenomenality Science is, and must remain, of immense interest to those who are themselves fully identified with the phenomenal, but it is entirely unreliable—because *basically* fictitious—as an explanation of our relation to the universe which appears to surround us and to which we appear to belong.

The metaphysical development of philosophy alone can reveal—even though it may never be able to state in dualistic terms—what ultimately we are and what is our relation to our phenomenal universe, inseparable from ourselves, a revelation which the most optimistic could hardly anticipate from the empirical methods of Science.

46 - The "Rights of Man"—A Dialogue

WHAT IS the truth concerning these "Rights of Man" that I read so much about?

Is there any?

Is there any—what?

Truth.

Don't see how there could be, but is there?

Who gave Man anything of the kind?

I suppose some people would answer that it was God.

The evidence for such an origin comes from Man himself.

Then Man gives himself his rights?

Man sells his newspapers by telling himself day after day, week after week, month after month, year after year, what a hero he is. You are enough of a psychologist to know the power of propaganda.

Then he is not a hero either?

In his own eyes he is, no doubt—by now—the hell of a hero.

And he has no rights?

Have other sentient beings any rights?

Not that I know of—unless it be the right to kill other sentient beings.

Very well, then; what rights can Man have that other sentient beings have not?

I cannot imagine any. But he exercises the right to kill, if right it be, in a more trigger-happy and wholesale manner than all the rest put together.

Does that distress you?

Yes, it does!

Then you are an ass! He does what he does, like the rest. Perhaps he has to. If you wish to blame him, his blame lies in his attempt to justify his abominations, not in the abominations themselves.

Then you agree that the "Rights of Man" are all my eye?

I think too highly of your eye to agree. They are chemically-pure balderdash!

But seriously—technically—what *are* they?

Rights? What could they be but a legal fiction?

Why "fiction"?

Why? Who could there be to have any?

ꟹ

The question of whether you exist or do not exist does not arise: you are not *there* to do either.

There can be no question of whether an "I" exists or does not exist: *there is no kind* of "I" to have either positive or negative existence.

47 — *Abolition*

I

THE POINT is not whether "things" as such exist or do not exist as objects, but whether their *subject* exists or does not exist.

This can best be visualised by asking "who is there to exist as subject of 'things' that either exist or do not exist?"

If we are able to apperceive that there cannot be an entity that either exists or does not exist, i.e. that could have any kind of existence, positive or negative, that could be either objectively present or objectively absent as an entity—then no "things" can have either existence or non-existence.

Conceptually any thing and every thing can exist that has a subject, but the subject of every such object is itself a conceptual object—which must have a subject and so on *ad infinitum.*

Therefore no object, or absence of object, can exist—otherwise than as a concept in mind, for no subject is available that is not also a concept.

Does not this point directly at the immanent transcendence

that is non-finite intemporality?

II

"Things" could not exist apart from their subject.

No object can have apparent independent existence.

Appearance, whatever form it may take, being objectification of what objectifies it, is inseparable from its objectifier.

Therefore object and subject are devoid of duality, different only as concepts, the one conceived as see-er, the other as what is seen, hearer and heard, toucher and touched, thinker and thought.

Neither has any sort or kind of being apart from the other, and as "one" both are uncognisable and phenomenally inexistent as anything whatever.

Noumenon (mind) manifesting itself objectively by this mechanism of appearance is non-duality extended and rendering itself perceptible in an imagined context of space and duration.

Such spatio-temporal context is integral in every sensorial perception and, like the divided concepts it makes manifest, is an expression of noumenality, both transcendent and immanent.

"A perception, sudden as thinking, that subject and object are one, will lead to a deeply mysterious wordless understanding: and by this understanding will you awake to the truth of Chan." (Huang Po, *Wan Ling Record*)

Note: "The Truth of Ch'an" is a homologue for "enlightenment."

Any action based on the notion of an independent

autonomous entity necessarily implies failure to understand the fundamental revelation of all esoteric religion, and of metaphysical apprehension.

48 ·- All About Us—A Dialogue

I

Hullo! You look worried; what's up?

Not worried, just angry!

What a waste of good energy! What about?

You.

Me? Waste indeed! Who said what?

Chap said that you were bogus!

Chap presumably knows what he is talking about. So I am. Whyever not?

No one was ever less bogus, whatever else you may be!

So I am not, but all the whatever elses instead.

What on Earth are *you* talking about? How can you be all sorts of things, including contradictions?

My dear chap, as "myself" I am exactly nothing; as whatever I am perceived to be—I appear.

I thought that was just a theory, but you are taking it as a fact!

It is as much a fact as anything in phenomenal manifestation can be so called. Whatever could there be for me to be?

Are you trying to persuade me that you have no personal character or identity whatever?

No persuasion is being used; I am merely asking you whatever you imagine I could possibly be, and how?

You yourself must know what you yourself are!

My perceptual and conceptual interpretation of my appearance is as valid, or invalid, phenomenally, as that of any other observer. One's own is apt to be a bit more flattering, but equally imaginary.

Well, how do you see yourself?

I have so many "selves" that I have never tried to count them, some quite unfit for respectable society. Our dreams give us a wider range than our waking-dream because less inhibited.. We only judge those in retrospect, and according to "waking" standards: while dreaming we accept ourselves for whatever we seem to be.

And you accept what other people think of you in the same spirit?

Surely anything else would be absurd? Whatever people "think" of me is their *thought, visualised in their own aspect of mind or "memory" as it is called; what could it have to do with me? With what I am, or with what I am not?*

So you don't care what they think?

Do I appear in your mind as such an ass as to care about what goes on in a reflection of split-mind? I am neither what they think nor what I think: thought as a mental image. Damn it, am I only an image in mind?

Come to think of it—perhaps you are that *also?*

Phenomenally *I could not be anything else. Nor could anyone, any phenomenon.*

Phenomenally, then, we are only what is perceived?

Perceived and conceived: the word says it! There is very precisely nothing else we could possibly be.

As such we are the objects of a "self" or subject, itself an object, an "other" to a self? And there aren't any?

As images in mind they are innumerable, but they can have no factual existence whatever.

Because where there is no "self" there cannot be "others" either? We have no "self," so that. . . .

Our supposed "self" is what "others" conceive—and "others" include our own self-conceiving.

So that each of us is an "other"?

A supposed "other," supposed by a supposed "self." "Others" are images in mind: They have no "self" and no "otherness."

That means that as "others" we too are that?

Of course.

So that we too have neither self nor otherness?

There is no "self" and no "other": they are merely the mechanism of dualist manifestation via a subject and its object.

"We" are an effect of the splitting of mind by a time-factor?

That is so—every object is "other" to its subject; what we commonly think we are *is just "other" to whatever is perceiving it.*

None of whom exists as such?

None.

Then what are we all?

Just plain—very, very, plain—I, forever unaware of what I-ness is. Until you have deeply seen that this must be so you are necessarily in "bondage."

II

Re-considering what we were discussing this morning it might perhaps be difficult to see how it could be otherwise.

In fact what could we be as appearances but concepts in split-mind—our own concepts and those of apparent "others"?

Was that news to you? Have not Sages, Prophets, and men of vision, even philosophers, been telling you that since their words were recorded in writing several millenia ago in conceptual "time"?

They have, but we weren't able to believe it.

Did they ask you to believe it? Do you need to believe it? Can't you see for yourself that it could not possibly be otherwise?

But so-perceived how do "selves" act?

They do not act. That also was told to us several millenia ago, though not explained in our own idiom. They appear to re-act, which is quite another matter.

Also as images in mind?

Of course.

Then what is what they appear to do?

A conceptual interpretation of such re-acting.

But what is re-acting?

An apparent functioning, called yü wei *in Chinese. Our "living."*

Ultimately there must be something behind mere appearance in mind?

Undoubtedly.

Then what is that?

It is not "that": it is "this" if you must point towards it. The Taoists describe it more accurately than anyone else.

As what?

Let us try to apperceive it by saying that it is a functioning called wu wei—*which implies "not-reacting."*

But what is functioning?

Wait a moment. That functioning, to continue Taoist terminology, is called wei wu-wei—*"an acting (which is) not-reacting." That is* prajña.

Can't we say it in our own language?

We have understood too little to have words for it. Let us try, by saying that it is transcendent noumenality, immanent as phenomenality, objectifying what it is as what we appear to be by means of dualistic manifestation.

But the acting? The functioning?

That seems *to occur, but all occurrence is only in mind.*

Then, how does it work?

By the conceptual extension of three directions of measurement from our source, which constitutes what we call volume in "space," accompanied by a further direction of measurement or supervolume, which is interpreted by our psychic apparatus as "time" and which measures the apparent duration of three-dimensional volume.

None of which *is,* or is real?

Such words mean nothing—or what they mean is not this. It neither is nor is not—as the Masters said, it is neither real nor unreal. I am seeking to describe in dualistic language what is not dual.

But where do we come in?

"We," as what "we" are, have never been out—for "we" are all that is. There is not anything else but what we are.

And yet we are nothing!

As appearance in mind—yes. But, being nothing as appearance, we are everything as what-we-are.

We are both source and what appears to be?

Neither and both. Noumenon and phenomenon are not two, nor are they different, nor are they any "thing." What they are is transcendence phenomenally, and immanence noumenally. No more has ever been said, or could be—as far as my poor understanding goes.

Would it satisfy religious people?

Probably not.

They are just plain wrong, suffering from auto-hallucination?

Not as I see it. They may be quite right, though their way, being a positive one, may be long and ineffective.

How so?

May I say that they are not "seeing" it by apperception, but "feeling" it by affectivity? The approaches are different, but neither need be wrong, and neither must be right.

So it may be as glorious as they believe it must be?

Whyever not? There is plenty of reason to suppose that it may be so.

But are they not projecting upon it dualistic emotions?

They do that continually, but the mutual negation of positive and negative affectivity may well be represented by something ultimately indescribable but of which such words as "beatitude," "benediction," and "bliss"—three "B's"—may represent a reflection in duality.

And it cannot be known at all?

I can only think of one word that might suggest it.

Which is. . . .

A strange word really, when you consider it. Cannot you guess of what I am thinking?

Grace?

Precisely!

49 ~ Does "Existence" Exist?

"EXISTENCE" IS a conceptual objectivisation (of some "thing" that *is* or appears to *be*). In the abstract, i.e. not objectively applied, it has no meaning.

"Existence" thus is a concept relative to "non-existence."

If "existence" were taken to imply "appears to be, or *appears* to have being," it would then become equated with "appearance," cease to denote whatever object appears, and all appearance could be said to exist. But that would be a contradiction-in-terms, for "appears to exist" implies its opposite "does not appear to exist," which requires potential non-apparent existence.

Therefore "apparent" existence cannot connote existence as such.

"Existence" and its opposite "non-existence" remain objective and relative concepts, so that whatever is said to exist or not to exist must necessarily be an object in mind.

An object, however, is by definition apparent, and what cannot be apparent cannot be an object. It follows that what is objective may exist, but that what is not objective cannot exist.

Therefore though objectivity may exist, subjectivity does not.

In short "you" may be thought to exist—either conceptually

or materially—because "you" are my object, but I do not exist as "I" because, as I, I am your subject. I could only exist as I if I were an object, but an object cannot be subject, or subject an object, so that as subject I cannot exist.

Therefore, as I, no thing (object) exists, but things (objects) may appear to exist, and their subject neither exists nor appears to exist.

Existence as such is a conceptual illusion, an appearance in mind only.

50 ~ *The Answer—A Dialogue*

I am disinclined to believe in a phenomenal subject of phenomenal objects.

Yes? Then how many subjects are you?

What do you mean? Every object must have a subject.

What is an object?

Well—a concept in mind.

Is that "an object"?

It is an objectification at least.

Let us choose our words carefully: it is an objecti-visation—*but not "an object"—something "seen," not something "made."*

But something "seen" needs a "see-er."

That is the apparent mechanism of dualism, but there is none: there is only a "see-ing"—no "see-er" and no thing "seen."

You mean that there is no phenomenal "subject" of phenomenal "objects," for they and the see-er of them are the see-ing?

Of course; surely that is axiomatic?

Then there are no objects?

None whatever: no such thing *has ever existed.*

So that no subject is needed?

None whatever.

There has never been any subject at all?

A "subject" is just an invention, a theoretical entity devised in order to account for supposed objects.

Then what objecti*fies* all appearance?

Whatever do you mean? I do, of course!

51 - "Existence" in Vedanta

SRI ATMANANDA quotes, source not stated:
"The non-existence of the non-existent is existence itself."
and also:
"Existence of the non-existent disproves non-existence."

That is the Positive Way *desperately* trying to remain positive. Significantly he gives the quotations without source or comment. Analysis would have involved the Negative Way.

But there is neither positive nor negative existence that is other than conceptual. Both existence and nonexistence are modes of existence, as the quotation itself asserts, but it is the *absence of both* that constitutes the truth he is inseeing.

Why is that? Because existence as such—any kind of existence, positive or negative—is conceptual and therefore phenomenal: only their mutual extinction is noumenon, only their absence is noumenal presence.

Split-mind must be in abeyance if whole-mind is to function as "whole," and then such functioning phenomenally is negative functioning, and cannot directly be revealed via dualistic thought or its verbal expression.

The profoundly analytical mind of Atmananda, perhaps the purest Vedantic dialectician since Sankara, teaching positive Vedanta, forbears to confuse his devotees. Perhaps also, to him, it could not matter whether the "truth" is to be apprehended positively or negatively, and in fact it does not matter to anyone who has understood—for what the dualistic word "truth" stands for is neither the one nor the other, and only the approach is in question.

52 ~ *The Infamous Void*

IT SEEMS difficult to understand why it is considered necessary to assume that only the objective makes sense, why the wearisome, and surely ludicrous, attempt goes on, goes on and on, to objectivise the non-objective, which is so evidently impossible. Torturing language and simile, in order objectively to describe this which can have no objective quality whatever, could never succeed, and every sentence defeats its own ends.

Wherein lies the difficulty of apperceiving the non-objective? Conditioned we are to objectivisation, by education and habit, but need it take long to adapt to the verisimilitude, let alone the inevitability, of the necessary counterpart of the objective? Should not one moment's silence of the mind suffice?

Objectivisation posing as the only truth, as an undisputed act of faith, a sacred and unquestionable dogma, as a spell whose binding at all costs must not be broken, is surely just a superstition, a superstition appertaining only to science.

Inevitably and always, this objectivisation arrives at something called "the void" or "emptiness," an object still—some *thing* that is empty—although there is nothing there! How futile all this is, traditional though it may be! An object that is no object! What a result! Are we really conditioned into such a state of psychic paralysis that we are incapable of apperceiving what this must necessarily be, without all these elaborate dialectics that point steadily in the opposite direction?

Making this a mystery is making "this" an obscure object: whereas what-this-is is much more obvious than any object could ever be; an object is always over there—and the whereabouts of "this" is very precisely here; an object is only in one place, whereas the situation of "this" is ubiquitous; true, "this" is objectively absent, but non-objectively "this" is eternally present.

"We" don't have to look in order to "see" that "this" is wherever "we" happen to be.

53 · The Question—A Dialogue

"Do you exist, or not?" The eternal question.

There is no answer.

Why not?

It is not a question.

But it is!

A question is only such in relation to an answer.

Then why is there no answer to this question?

Because it is based on false premises.

How so?

It assumes that there is an I either to exist or not to exist. Since there is not, could not be, an objective I, which would constitute a contradiction in terms, how can there be a question about its positive or negative existence?

Then you have only to answer "'I' do not exist!"

That begs the question: answering implies someone to exist.

So then you do exist!

That "you" begs the same question.

I do not understand.

This which I am *neither exists nor does not exist; I* have *neither*, know *neither*, *cannot be* known to have *or* not to have *either*, *positive or negative existence.*

So what?

No such question as yours can arise.

54 ·- Facing the Facts

(a) There cannot be a Path, because there is no "where" to go, and no "one" to go anywhere.

Only an objective "me" could "do" that, or anything else, and such are merely figments in mind.

(b) There cannot be "enlightenment" at the end of a non-existent "path," because there is no such entity as a "me" to have it, and "enlightenment"—if the term means anything in this context—implies all that, non-objectively, I am, have always been, always shall be, unobscured by the space-time extension in which my figment appears. Therefore there is no thing to be acquired and no one to acquire it.

(c) There cannot be anything to "do," because do-ing is an action, and act-ing is subject to the concept of duration. Duration, called "time," has no factual existence, is not a "thing" but a dimension, a direction of measurement. Like volume, called "space," it is an interpretation of noumenal non-objectivity, the intemporal phenomenal absence which is what we are as I.

Act-ing, a temporal phenomenon, cannot possibly as such affect its noumenon which is transcendent, and whose immanence phenomenality is, for noumenon as such is what is implied by the term "intemporality."

So what may be stated? Is it not unavoidably evident that all we could be must be noumenal, and that what we appear to be cannot be anything but phenomenal, since to suppose that there could be anything else would manifestly be absurd? Since, therefore, our every phenomenal action and experience is an expression of our noumenality, we can assume that the Great Masters knew what they were talking about, and that they meant what they said.

We can take their words literally—or we can do so whenever they are fairly correctly reported—and avoid employing our illusory volition in endeavouring to do the opposite.* To what end? There is neither end nor beginning, neither death nor birth: there is only This, Here, Now—as we may try to express it in our dualistic lingo, which was just what they were trying to point out in theirs.

There is no mystery in this, of course. Japanese teachers of archery and swordsmanship know it well, as do some

---

* To read what is written, in books and articles; to listen to what is said, in lectures and discussions; to watch what is being done, in classes or in private, one would have to assume that no-one, no-one at all, teacher or pupil, had ever heard of, let alone read, the Great Masters. Yet they spoke clearly, simply, directly, and even translations by philologists who have only a vague notion of the meaning of what they are academically translating, cannot disguise it.

Do all these people imagine that the T'ang-dynasty Masters did not know what they were talking about, did not mean what they said, or have they never read them? Perhaps they think they know better? At any rate they nearly all seem to preach and to do precisely the opposite.

Western teachers of therapy: people do what their conditioning (call it "ego" if you *must*) has inured them to *feel* is right for *them*—even though they may be told that it is wrong, even shown that it is wrong, even though—sometimes—they *know* that it is wrong. Conditioned or reflex action is difficult indeed to overcome!

But surely it is *that* which needs method, practice, and every sort of "gimmick," to eradicate—and not the simple facing-up to what we are. Are they not training, even sometimes consecrating, themselves to *reinforce* their *resistance* to sitting in a *Bodhimandala*—which means laying themselves open to the truth of letting themselves be dreamed by what they are?

55 ~ Note on Noumenon

LET US not forget that the presence of noumenality in phenomenality is only cognisable as absence: we cannot be sensorially aware of its presence as noumenon, since it is what we are.

Thus sensorial absence of noumenality is its noumenal presence, and it cannot be anything but what we ourselves are who seek to conceptualise it. Hence we can say that noumenal presence is phenomenal absence, and noumenal absence is phenomenal presence.

Regarded conceptually they are mutually exclusive. But noumenon, as the being of all experience (phenomenal) cannot have any empirical existence whatever as noumenon. Hence noumenon can metaphorically be said to "speak" as being *or* as non-being, as being-conscious *or* as being-unconscious, for both, like speaking itself, are phenomenal manifestations. As regards "itself" noumenality cannot "say" or "do" anything—for "it" is no "thing" and cannot be conceived at all, since "conceiving" as such is all that "it" is as what we are.

Noumenon, if we like to say it, is all imaginable presence, itself absence, and also all imaginable absence (total absence of all "things"), itself presence. But "itself" is neither presence nor absence, for both connote "time" and "space" the existence of which is phenomenal (apparent) only, and as such it can have no "self."

In short, if total phenomenal absence is what noumenon is, dualistically conceived, total phenomenal presence is what it is also, apprehended as whole-mind.

Note: Subject and object can never phenomenally be "one," and noumenally they can never be two. But noumenally they cannot be "one" either—for "one" is a conceptual object, and noumenon knows none such, not even "itself" as such, for all that "it" is, has ever been, or ever could be, is total phenomenality.

56 ·– Surely the Answer Is . . .

SURELY THE answer is that the Buddha, having found himself awake to the obvious fact that this phenomenality was only an objectivisation in mind, he thereby immediately became aware of his phenomenal inexistence?

His compassionate heart then wept for all those sentient-beings believing in their personal existence and bearing the appalling burden of responsibility for their every gesture.

Ministers of State, believing themselves to be responsible for their country and everyone in it, utterly conditioned without being aware of it, ordinary men believing themselves responsible for their wives and families, businesses, and everything that to them appeared to depend on whatever they did or did not do—what an intolerable burden they all bore from morning till night, until far into the night! Of course he wept! Of course he saw it all as "suffering"! Only heartless cynics, like ourselves, and the Chinese, can just laugh!

Why do we laugh instead of cry? Because, after all, it is a laughing, not a crying, matter! A dream is only a dream, a nightmare only a nightmare—however agreeable or disagreeable either may *seem* to be while it is being *experienced* in space-time. But experience belongs only to the dream and the dreamed. When there is no one to experience dreams and nightmares, sleeping or waking, who is there either to laugh or to cry?

57 ~ *The Conceptual Universe*

I

EVERY QUALIFICATION of every noun, and consequently every quality whatsoever attributed to any object, is a concept in mind, in the context of previous concepts of the same order.

Every noun, qualified or not, is also a concept in mind. In consequence, nominally and adjectivally, all objects are conceptual.

Verbally, whether "he," "she," "it," "you," or "they" be addressed, each becomes a conceptual object. There remain the personal "I" and "we" in the subjective cases.

If in either case the "I" or "we" speaking be conceived as phenomenal objects, then they too are concepts in mind. Only in the event of the letter "I" being used as a sound or symbol expressing impersonal noumenality could it be maintained that a concept in mind is not present—and the likelihood of such condition is not normally in question.

Therefore, excluding the latter possibility, everything we say, everything we write, everything we think, is a concept in mind reinforcing previous concepts preserved in memory, and that must automatically apply to everything we read, everything we hear, see, taste, touch, smell, and cognise.

Is it not evident from this simple analytical statement that the sensorially perceptible universe must necessarily be a conceptual universe, and that its sole and total apparent existence can only be as a conceptual phenomenon in mind?

Has no one ever thought of this before? Surely, but whoever he may have been, and however many they may have been, innumerable no doubt, they seem to have kept very quiet about it? Not, of course that the sutras and the recorded words of nearly all the great sages have not implied it, but the circumstances of their times seem to have caused them to indicate it less directly. Perhaps Nagarjuna, Arya Deva, Candrakirti, etc. in the Madhyamika said it clearly, often, and in much greater detail? Yes, so why not read them? No one is ever likely to say it again so thoroughly as they did—though perhaps in so much greater detail that in a general sense it no longer seemed obvious?

II

But even so its evidence might not seem to be conclusive if we continued to regard it in the untenable context in which space-time is tacitly accepted as some kind of permanent factuality within which everything occurs or appears to occur. Unless we have clearly apperceived that spatial extension is a functional element of all perceiving, and that duration accompanies it as a dimension interpreted as "lasting," without which process nothing whatever could be perceived or conceived, the conceptuality of the universe and of the conceiver of it might not be seen as rigorously inevitable.

The universe does not appear in an everlasting context of permanent space-time extension; it comes into apparent or conceptual existence simultaneously with the spatial and temporal extension which render it apparent and available for conceiving. And, finally, *its perceiving is essentially singular whereas its conceiving is apparently plural.*

When this is clearly apprehended it should no longer be possible to doubt the perfectly conceptual nature of the sensorially perceived universe and of the "conceiver" of it.

Without understanding the nature of space-time, the instantaneous and "quantic" extension thereof in the apparently continuous process of temporal objectivisation, it will always be difficult for us of "to-day" to apprehend the veritable nature of the conceptual universe.

Note: In case it should be suggested that objects might be thought to exist as such in their own right, i.e. objects as being independent of their subject, it should only be necessary to point out that in Buddhist and other metaphysics it is axiomatic that they can not and do not so exist. Moreover the aforesaid Nagarjuna and his school of Madhyamika have proved from every angle not only the evident impossibility but the absurdity of such a notion.

58 ~ Quips and Queries - III

Memories are not of actions, but of reactions.

❧

When the sun shines is it we who "break through" the clouds to the sun, or the sun which breaks "through" the clouds to us, without warning?

❧

There is only one question—and the asking is the answer.

❧

"We" are effects, not causes.

❧

Saying it simply: *There is no phenomenal way out.*

❧

Offended? Only an object can suffer offence (or any other emotion). Could I be an object?

❧

Non-volitional action *(wu-wei)* causes no reaction.
Why? Because it is non-action.
Reaction is dependent on action.

There cannot be either self nor other,
For there is no self that is not other,
Nor any other that is not self.

PART IV

The Conceptual Universe - 2

Apparently absent in Relativity,
I am present Absolutely

59 · Almost Everybody Who Writes . . .

ALMOST EVERYBODY who writes books or articles on metaphysical matters writes from the point of view of a bound, identified, and supposedly autonomous individual, and in apparently full acceptance of the notion that such is what he is.

Whatever could be the use of deliberately writing from a position of ignorance? To what could it lead, what possibility could there be of it revealing any non-dual understanding?

If we are unable to write as from whole-mind, in so far as that may be done via the relativity of language, what result could our writing have but that of misleading our fellow-prisoners? Anything but writing from knowledge of what we are must surely add to the burden of our mutual bondage? How could it fail to do that?

Is it so difficult to *know* what we are? Can we not speak and write from *this* knowledge instead of from *that* ignorance which is belief in the false knowledge of what we are not—even if *this* knowledge is not fully integrated in buddheity?

One has the impression that writers imagine that it is expected of them to write as from incomprehension instead of from comprehension. Perhaps they are shy, and feel that it is pretentious to do otherwise? But to what do they think they would be pretending? Knowledge is not pretension. If they *were* Buddhas—do Buddhas write at all?

If we have something to say, and believe that it is worth saying, that can only be so if it seeks to express pure apprehending. The expression of that from behind prison bars can only delude the deluded whose delusion is that there are bars and that there is anyone to be in gaol.

Note: This has no bearing on conventional writing about matters of theory, of practice, of history, discussion of any kind, for these concern exclusively the affairs of the space-time continuum and are not in themselves "metaphysical matters."

60 · "The Buddha Taught . . ."

I

THE FAMILIAR statement that every object is empty (*k'ung* in Chinese, *sunyu* in Sanscrit), that no object has any nature of its own, "own-being" or "self-nature" in English, implies that it lacks objective existence. This means that all it is is the perceiving of it, that it is nothing in itself, but only what is apparently perceived. This has been known from the earliest times, and this understanding is common to the esoteric aspect of all the great religions, being fundamental in Buddhism, Vedanta, and Sufism.

Everyone who studies any of these doctrines must be familiar with it, but its application to daily living, which surely must be the essential application, is rarely more than tentative.

What, then, does it imply when applied to ourselves? It not only implies, it states, that there can be no such factuality as an entity anywhere in our space-time universe, and that we ourselves do not, and could not, exist at all as such. This, also, is axiomatic, has often been stated, but is rarely faced as a fact.

When we apply it we find that a sentient-being in space-time is nothing but an image in mind, has no existence of its own whatever, but is only an appearance perceived and conceived by the "subject" of each such perception and conception, each such "subject" being also an object similarly perceived and conceived by other apparent conceived percepts.

This requires that a single source of perceiving perceives via multiple percepts, each and every such percept being conceived as an entity via which each and every other percept is in turn perceived and conceived, no example of which has any kind of personal existence of its own or in its own right.

That this is so we need have no doubt whatever. Probably every established sage in each of the great religions has known it, and has made it clear, each in his own way, that so it is; and if we have understood what they have told us, we must have reached this apprehension ourselves and should be satisfied that it is the truth and that no other interpretation of the facts could be possible.

Each of "us," then, is only, can only be, whatever is perceived, and is conceptually interpreted as being. Ourselves, we are nothing whatever; as such we simply are not, as autonomous entities we do not exist at all. It is not we who perceive and conceive one another or ourself, for there is no "we": we and they are perceived, conceived, and interpreted via one another, one such so-rendered-apparent and supposed "other" being each of "ourselves."

II

Is this a shock? If so, it proves the depth of our conditioning in the illusion of autonomous individuality, which also constitutes our so-called "bondage." Incidentally this is why "bondage" is known to be an illusion also—for the sufficient reason that there has never been any entity to be "bound."

What, then, does this imply in practice, in space-time "living"? It implies that objectively you are only what is perceived, conceived, and interpreted via other sentient-beings, one of whom is what you are conditioned to regard as "myself"; as an object you have a variable appearance, relatively unfavourable when interpreted via your "enemies," favourable when interpreted via your "friends," and usually a pretty fine guy, or a grand girl, when interpreted via "yourself." In fact, however, you are exactly no thing whatsoever, *k'ung, sunya, totally devoid of objective existence,* and merely an appearance, a phenomenon in "mind" or "consciousness," of absolutely no fixed identity, quality, or attributes.

Subjectively, on the other hand, you are also totally devoid of identity, quality, or attributes, and you merely represent phenomenally the subjective faculty which produces all phenomenality and "manifestation." As such you are "I," as I am "I," as every sentient-being, human, animal, insectival and vegetable is "I," and I can have no objective existence whatever, for the accusative of "I," is not "me," as currently misunderstood, but always and only "you."

III

One may well ask why it is considered necessary to go on hinting at this, pointing to it, saying it obscurely, partially, making a holy mystery of it? Nearly all the greater scriptures and recorded sayings of the Masters and Prophets, and many poets, are bursting at the seams with it. Indeed it constitutes in itself the truth, the whole truth, and nothing but the truth, in so far as such a thing as "truth" there can be, and its complete apprehension leaves little that could be regarded as essential to be understood, for nearly all that remains unsaid follows from it or is forever unsayable. In bygone days and in other lands, when there were Masters almost everywhere available, as in India and China, it may indeed have been desirable to reserve this essential understanding for those who were mature and ripe to receive it, and so to instruct them that each apperceived it for himself only at the moment when its apprehension should be most efficacious. But such conditions do not obtain to-day in the West, and what does obtain is confusion universal and confounded. It is read and re-read, hinted at or obscurely stated, but rarely if ever understood.

We have no Masters, the *Guru* is always within anyhow; if we state it in plain words the *Guru* within will reveal its absolute and ultimate verity to those who are able to receive it.

Perhaps, so-stated, you reject it absolutely, perhaps you laugh at it, dismiss it with scorn? That some readers may do so does not seem improbable at all. All are not likely to be ready for it. But why are such readers not ready for it? One may suggest that the reason is that they have been led astray into by-paths of illusion and nonsense, based on their own precious supposedly-autonomous individual entities, that they are ironclad and impervious to the esoteric facts, and deaf to the essential truth that all the great Masters so patiently, so pertinaciously, so deviously sought to reveal to them.

IV

Perhaps you are confused because I seem to be writing here about ourselves as entities just as we all do? I have to do that because I am as we all are, and I could not possibly do otherwise. Apparent and suppositious entities "we" are, and "living" at all entails the apparent living of this double life. But we can recognise its dual character, and that is what is required.

That we are apparent entities is obvious and undeniable,

and that superficially we all appear to act like entities is evident also. All this is due to the fact that our dualist universe is a phenomenal creation of divided mind, perceived objectively by pseudo-subjects which are objectivised as "selves," and our living in that universe, including our thought and its expression, is based on relativity, which is the comparison of opposing concepts.

Moreover, understanding "what-we-are-not" merely *indicates* to us what we are, for split-mind cannot cognise its own wholeness, and the wholeness of mind cannot reason by division, and cannot use words which depend upon relativity which it knows not. Living, we have to accept our dualist limitations, which means that although we can apprehend the truth about what we are, it is not within our power to think or speak directly as whole-mind, and anyhow no conceivable speech could convey it. Speaking as apparent entities in order to demonstrate that we are not such, illogical as it seems, is a limitation inherent in our phenomenal duality.

As an object, no doubt, I am only an imaginary dummy on which observers hang clothing, each of his own choice, or, if you prefer the simile, I am a mirror in which each sees his pseudo-self reflected without being aware of it. As an apparent entity in space-time, all that I can pretend to be is an apparently re-agent mechanism that finds expression in conation, which is the apparent activity of what is called "an ego." But are you asking me to believe in the factuality of all this? Could that really be what I am, what each of us is, what we are?

I am endeavouring to point out to you that it could not, that what we are, what we all are as "I," is what all the sages of all the ages have seen, understood, and tried to explain to us is what we are, always were, and will be forever. Since the "space" and "time" on which all these phenomenal notions depend are only the conceptual framework of their own conceptual existence, may we not say simply and frankly that no such question can be said to arise?

V

Is someone thinking about Napoleon or Plato, Shakespeare or Mozart? If so, he is just entifying as usual, and has not understood. Has he forgotten that "the Buddha taught for forty-nine years, but no word was spoken"? Unless that is understood it is difficult to see how the rest could be: it is a kind of key, universal, to the unlocked door.

Transposed, we can say that many battles were won by Napoleon, many plays were written by Shakespeare, concertos composed by Mozart, but no "Napoleon" ever fought a battle, no "Shakespeare" ever wrote a line, nor did any "Mozart" play a note of music.

Do we ever go far enough back, make the final negation of the negator of negating, take "the jump off the top of the hundred-foot pole"?

Do we exist or do we not exist?

There has never been anyone *either* to exist *or* not to exist.

There has never been "anyone" to answer such a question.

Note: Who made the final negation (of the negator of negating)? I did. In negating my ultimate objectivity I negated my "self." So doing I abolished the notion of "myself" as an object. Then nothing was left, for I am no thing. Objectively I remain represented by all phenomenality soever.

When negating negates the objectivised "negator" I negate an (objective) "self." Then no object remains, nor-therefore-any subject. Phenomena in their totality are manifested, but their noumenon as such has no objective existence.

Only that which is extended in space and time can have perceptual existence, so that apparent existence depends upon percepts. What we are is not what is conceived, but its conceiving, and "conceiving" cannot be its own object. It follows that what-we-are cannot be extended in space-time, and so cannot be conceived.

That is all that needed saying? Quite so.

Transcendence

> Quite impossible is it, even though we seek throughout the Three Regions (Past, Present, and Future) to find the Buddha elsewhere than in mind.
>
> PADMA SAMBHAVA, *Knowing Mind*

What we are is not an entity extended in space and in duration.

That is why "no words were ever spoken by the Buddha," etc.: "the Buddha" was not a "space-time entity."

I am not a "space-time entity" either: that is the difference between Nirvana and samsara, Noumenon and phenomena, Subjectivity and objectivity. What is implied by Tao, Godhead, Dharmakaya, etc. is not extended in spacetime: non-extension and extension is *the only difference* between Absolute and relative. It is also the apparent difference between Void and form, the "Realised," "Enlightened," "Liberated," and the "identified," the "ignorant," the "bound."

It is the difference between the Unconditioned and the conditioned. It is the difference between what I am, whatever we are subjectively, and the objectivised phenomena which are "born" and "die," between Intemporal-Infinity and apparent entities in space-time, between "Whole-Mind" and figments in mind that is split by duality.

The supposition of a "present" relative to a "past" and a

"future" is a psychic chain which binds us to *samsara,* the chain of space-time extension, based on sequential duration—which is Movement.

"That which has passed," "that which is to come," relative to "this which is (supposed to be) present," are the links in the horizontal chain of our imaginary "bondage."

Stepping out of "time" is breaking the chain which "binds" us, and freedom from the concept of sequence automatically removes the shackle of material extension in "space." What then remains—phenomenally imagined—is infinite intemporality—and this is all that we are as "I."

This eternality can never become actual while we regard "time" and "space" objectively: it obtains as Awareness when our relation with "time" and "space" becomes nonobjective—for then we apperceive that what they are, and all they are, is the dimensional mechanism of our own phenomenal manifestation.

❧

To say that there is only one subject is nonsense:
There is no subject at all.
"A" subject is an invention in order to account for an object.
But the object has no need of "a" subject (thereby an object),
For it is only a concept in mind.
All concepts are objectifications:
There has never been "an" object,
And so there can never have been "a" subject.
Who, then, objectifies all objective appearance?
I do.

61 ·- Dialectic Approach to Integration

I

IT MAY be said that there is only one thing that need be profoundly understood, without which no understanding could be valid, and from which—if that is completely comprehended—all else must necessarily follow.

That understanding is the total, and final, absence of oneself, that *as such* I never have existed, do not now exist, and never will exist, for I can have no being subject to "time."

II

Phenomena can have only an apparent space-time existence as concepts in mind.
Then who is there "completely to comprehend" this?
Nobody, I do.
As any sentient-being may say, if he apperceives that
Objective absence is subjective presence,
Which is absolute release.

III

Unless a self-supposed entity can abolish itself it cannot be liberated (since "liberation" is liberation from the idea of itself), but conversely, since it is self-supposed, unless it is liberated it cannot abolish itself. Such a problem appears to be insoluble; which comes first, the acorn or the oak-tree, the egg or the hen?

This is the answer: subject to the concept of sequential duration there can be no answer to a question posed in the form of a vicious circle, whereas un-subjected to the concept of "time" there can be no question.

In a time-context there can be no release, and no experienced occurrence of the liberation of a phenomenon can factually take place—since the experiencer has not any but an apparent existence and the imagined experience could only be a temporal illusion. Outside a time-context, unsubjected to any concept such as space-time, there can be no entity to be abolished, and nothing that is not liberation to be known.

Therefore the phenomenon does not abolish itself—since what-it-is is not phenomenal and noumenally can have no "self" to abolish—and so "it" cannot be liberated. And conversely, since noumenally there can be no "self" to be liberated, there cannot be any such event as "liberation" to occur in intemporality.

The concept itself is at fault, for—as the T'ang-dynasty Masters knew, the said "self-supposed entity" neither exists nor does not exist, never has nor ever will *either* exist *or* not-exist, so that all that "it" can be noumenally is the absence of its phenomenal non-existence. Therefore nothing whatsoever can factually occur to what is entirely phenomenal, the noumenality of which is transcendent to all concepts including those of "space" and "time" in which phenomena are necessarily extended.

IV

It may be said that noumenally there is—
Neither Here nor There,
Neither Now nor Then,
Neither This nor That.

These are axiomatic, and inclusive of all phenomenal manifestation.

The first abolishes opposing positions in Space, the second abolishes opposing positions in Time, the third abolishes opposing positions of Self and Other, and all three abolish opposing *positions* of the Thinker or Speaker in either space or time.

But the thinking *entity* as such remains intact. As subject it is removed from all three dimensions of Space, from Past, Present and Future, and from identification with Subject and Object, but it remains undisturbed as an entity, for it is *affirmed* as not being either of each of these pairs of interdependent counterparts.

In abolishing the relative positions of Space, Time, and Thinker, all remain as underlying concepts, and until these remaining objects are negated their subject remains intact.

That, no doubt, is why Shen Hui pointed out the inadequacy of the Masters' habitual formula "neither . . . nor . . ." and imposed a further negation, which he called the double absence or the double negative, "the negation of neither. . . nor. . . ." In these inclusive examples this will be the negation or abolition of no-Space and of no-Time whereby their subject-entity also is negated as having conceptual being, since the absence of no-Space and of no-Time is inconceivable. It should here be evident that as long as any conceptual object remains, the subject thereof can never be released.

The Chinese manner of expressing this "double negation," by negating the negative element of the initial negation, is apt to be confusing to us; therefore it is preferable here just to apply the word "absence" to the whole negation. In this case the formula becomes:

"We are required to apprehend the *absence* of 'neither Here nor There,' of 'neither Now nor Then,' of 'neither This nor That,' and thereby the absence of Space and of a conceiver of Space, of Time and of a conceiver of Time, of Self and of a conceiver of Self."

If we shall have apperceived these absences, in depth, we should thereby have apperceived our own objective absence, our total absence of *ens,* hereby we may apprehend that we can never know what we are—since we are nothing objective that could be known. Nor can we ever be conscious of what we are—since that is no "thing," and what is cognising cannot cognise what is cognising, any more than what is being conscious can be conscious of what is being conscious.

V

This apparent solution of continuity, speaking dialectically, between apparent events in a time-context and their intemporal noumenality should not be taken to imply separation—for there can be none; and the transcendence of the noumenal is surely the immanence of the phenomenal and vice-versa, as viewed from the one or the other standpoint.

Integration or re-integration undoubtedly "occurs," whereby as a result of a very rare equilibrium between normally excessive *positive* and normally deficient *negative* factors in a psyche—rendered possible by intensive negation—adjustments arise in that psyche.

Descriptions involving an access of "divine love," "universal compassion," "ecstatic happiness" and what-not, all affective manifestations, patently temporal and separated from their inseparable counterparts, are evidently phenomenal. What may be assumed to take place is simply that the phenomenon, suddenly relieved of its egoity, freed thereby from a burden of cares, pseudo-responsibilities, phobia and what-not, rebecomes normal, and by contrast with the worries of the living-dream feels as though gravity were no more, laughs hilariously perhaps, wishes to dance for joy and to embrace all phenomenal creation. And this is interpreted and recorded as "divine grace," universal benediction, and all the characteristics attributed to a *bodhisattva.*

But the remaining phenomenal events of that living-dream are not likely to be altered, and may continue to be those of a "saintly" as of a "sinful" personality—as Ramana Maharshi explained to us, though the phenomenon has, in a sense, become a "sage" in his understanding of what he is in relation to the apparent universe to which phenomenally he belongs. Serenity henceforward may well replace anxiety, for the basis of cares and worries has disappeared, and all that happens henceforward will appear different to what has happened in the past in that, whatever it may be, it will be seen as inevitable and as "right."

VI

Affectivity attributed to an "enlightened" sentient-being is a phenomenal manifestation of what sentience is, with its inevitable and inseparable counterpart, like that attributed to any "unenlightened" sentient-being, the origin of which is noumenal also. Any direct manifestation of noumenal "affectivity," if such were conceivable, would necessarily be intemporal and imperceptible as such in the sequence of duration. At most it could, perhaps, be represented by some impalpable "quality," recognisable in a time-sequence as "Grace" or "Serenity."

Sentience, let us not forget, is not "something" that "we" possess or experience, but is an indirect manifestation of what we *are.* If there could be any question of "possession" it would surely be sentience (what-we-are) that "possesses" what we think is "us"; the concept of a "self" is that of some "thing" which is sentient, and so "has" sentience, and such entity is entirely suppositional. This false identification, of course, is "bondage."

The apparent affectivity of an "enlightened" phenomenon is therefore not different from that of an "unenlightened" phenomenon since both are individualised representations in mind of the same "sentience." In a temporal context it must always and inevitably be thus, the "enlightenment" being simply the abolition of the inferential entity.

No dualistic emotion is thereby sublimated, for there is nothing in emotional counterparts to sublimate, and split affectivity (such as attraction and repulsion) remains "whole" in the unsplit mind of the intemporal. Therefore it cannot be supposed to manifest directly in an "enlightened" phenomenal object in a time-sequence as affectivity which as such is necessarily split. As a "wholeness" it cannot be phenomenally experienced, since *it is* what is experiencing phenomenally as subject and object. This immanence might conceivably be cognisable psychically in an "enlightened" phenomenon and be called "Grace," which should be the common noumenality of perceiver and perceived, and all that ultimately they are.

62 ·- The Way in Is the Only Way Out

I

WHENEVER ANY sentient-being makes an object of its space-time appearance, that object will necessarily appear as a "self," as an autonomous entity responsible for every one of its apparent actions; and a similar autonomy will be attributed to each other phenomenal "entity" so objectivised.

Such responsibility is entirely illusory, and it produces volition, which is the functional aspect of the notion of an "ego."

Conflict results, disharmony, and the "suffering" that is inherent in every moment of such a conceptual situation, "suffering" which is necessarily accompanied by its counterpart which, however romantically named and regarded, can never be anything but the negative aspect of "suffering" which is just *experience.*

Such is what is called "bondage," also "identification" (with an objective image in mind). Such also is its entirely illusory character.

This action on the part of any sentient-being must itself be an effect in temporality of apparent independence implying identification. That is so, and should be so understood. If no identification occurred no such autonomous action could occur either. But the aim of this brief Note is not to discuss the genesis of dualism, of the splitting of "mind"—which represents what we are—into subject and its objects which, as such, represent what we are not. The "Fall of Man," as described in the parable of the Garden of Eden or elsewhere, is an actuality to which we are already committed by apparent birth and by factual conditioning.

II

It follows that this situation could never be abolished by the self-same mechanism by which it came to appear, and on which its continuation in space-time depends. This means that the self-identified concept cannot abolish "itself" which is the concept of its own identity.

During the few thousand years of temporality of which records survive, many attempts have been made to find a solution to this problem, infinitely complicated "methods" and very simple "solutions," but if occasional success has been recorded no reliable or clearly-defined "way" has ever been found.

Summing up this long history of the struggle for "liberation" all that can be stated with finality is that sentient-beings must always appear as such, objectively extended in a space-time context, but that what they are non-phenomenally, other than as objectivised concepts, can never be either perceived or conceived since cognising cannot cognise what is cognising, and what is cognising is what they are.

Knowledge of this does not in itself constitute release from the apparent bondage of identification, but it surely constitutes an essential basis for such release.

III

What in fact sometimes transpires is, on the one hand, the apprehension that dialectic understanding of what-we-must-be does not itself break our misunderstanding whereby we believe we are what-we-are-not. On the other hand the dialectic understanding that what-we-are is not, and cannot be, anything objective at all, is indeed capable of producing a degree of conceptual negativity which, for an instant at least, may annihilate our false identification.

Then, if we already have the necessary understanding of what we must inevitably be, such understanding alone remains at that instant of apparent "time," and that imperfect dialectic understanding spontaneously re-becomes unitary or noumenal understanding that can never again be displaced. In fact split-mind has re-become whole.

The supposed autonomous individual is then no longer either individual or autonomous, and responsibility, dependent on that supposition, is no more. Knowing all that our appearance in space-time factually is, we remain what noumenally we are, and the "living dream" is dreamed in peace to its end.

The apparent difficulty of disidentification, which is reinforced by our conditioning in "time" from birth, derives from the fact that our subjective faculty is essentially what we are and perfectly valid when not personalised by identification with our phenomenality, our objective psycho-somatic appearance, and when freed from all conceptual attributions whatsoever. This means simply that we can all say "I," man and monkey, bull-dog and beetle, robin and rose, as long as we are not speaking as from any particularised phenomenon, subject of any object, object of any subject, cognisable in any way as any "thing," or in any manner limited by spatial or temporal concepts.

Uncognisable, what is cognising, we are nevertheless absolutely "I," but never can we know ourselves as anything whatever other than as the totality of objectivised phenomena none of which has any but conceptual existence as what "we" perceive and conceive as appearance.

❧

We can only dispose of objective "time" by becoming it, by knowing that phenomenally "we" are extended in it, that it is a dimension of our appearance, that it is "born" and "dies" with each of "us." Together we "fly."

It is an aspect of our "ego." Instead of reacting to it, or against it, "we" should be "with it," like our clocks and watches.

Noumenally it is still what we are—as Eternity.

Intemporal, Infinite, I am time and space.
Infinite, I am space; Intemporal, I am time,
For I am the extension of form, and its duration.

63 ⁓ LLANFAIRPWLLGWYNGYLLGOGERYCHWYR-NDROBWLL'LLANTYSILIOGOGOGOCH—A Dialogue

Hullo! You look as though you want something?

I do.

What is it?

Help.

Nothing like that to be had here. Only suggestions.

They'll have to do!

So what?

People tie me up.

Too bad! How?

They ask me whether I really believe that I do not exist.

And you assure them that you do not?

Not caught as easily as that!

Then what do you say?

That I neither exist nor do not exist. Is not that right?

Nothing can be right, but it is more classical.

Perhaps, but then they want to know who *neither exists nor does not exist.*

And who does, or doesn't?

That is what I want you to tell me.

Answers worth having come from within, not from without.

Very well then, pull them out; that is what I have come for!

I am not a dentist. But their question is not who else exists or does not, but "Who is saying that, who is speaking?"

He neither exists nor does not exist either.

How many of you are there who neither exist nor do not exist?

None. Nobody does anything whatever.

Neither somebody nor nobody?

No sort of body at all!

Neither entity nor non-entity?

No sort of entity whatever!

What sort of a body is a no-body?

He is a conceptual body.

And a non-entity?

He also is a concept. Then there is no difference between a somebody and a no-body, between a man and a concept?

A man is a concept, as also is a beetle—and every other object.

But a man is alive—one can touch him: a no-man cannot be touched.

Both "being alive" and "what is touched" are conceptual also.

"Touching" is a sense-perception.

Sentience—visual, auditory, tactile, gustatory, olfactory—is the basis of phenomena of the so-called "animate" variety, and the interpretation of a sense-perception is a concept.

So that there is no difference between a man-concept and a no-man concept, or any other affirmation and denial?

Phenomenally—as a result of relative interpretation—the difference appears to be absolute: noumenally—since both are just concepts in mind—there can be no difference, for nowhere is there a "thing" to be different from another "thing."

And whatever is conceptual exists in mind only, whether a sensorial concept like a man or a psychic concept like an angel?

Precisely.

And nothing non-conceptual exists, or seems to exist, at all either?

There cannot be anything that is other than conceptual.

Why is that?

What is not conceptual could not even *appear* to exist, even if such a thing could be, which obviously it cannot.

So that in fact whatever is cognisable—knowable at all—is thereby a concept?

Evidently.

But what about pure sense-perceptions anterior to interpretation as concepts?

They are presented by a complicated mechanism of cellular changes of a chemical nature, nerve-impulses, conditioned reflexes, articulations, etc., basically unrelated to the resulting conceptual image.

Then on what is the resulting image based?

It is based on "memory," which is said to be an accumulation of successive superimposed and related conceptual images, interpreted and reinterpreted, constantly varying and deteriorating, somewhat incredibly conserved by traces which are termed "engrams," in cellular matter called "the cerebellum"—all, of course, in a consecutive time-context.

So that there is, in fact, exactly no evidence, no reason whatever to suppose that what is so conceived has any factual resemblence to what was apparently perceived?

Can you see any?

As an image—no.

If not as an image?

Surely the interpretation, however arrived at, must have the same origin as the perception itself?

That would be my surmise also.

So that, in any event, there is nothing there, or anywhere, but "mind" only.

Then there is nothing at all left on your hands?

No, nothing!

Nothing left on whose hands?

Damn it all, can't I get rid of myself, dispose of my own existence? A chap must speak if he is required to argue!

How can a chap get rid of what he says does not exist?

You are as bad as the rest of them!

Is it not because he does not exist that he is unable to say, and so to know, that he does not exist?

That seems to strike home! Difficult to see through all the same. . . .

Perhaps the rest of them are right, has that ever occurred to you?

Then I cannot get rid of myself?

You can be rid of an objective "self," but you cannot be rid of whatever is doing whatever you appear to do.

Then how can I answer?

You cannot. Don't you know the old Scriptures, how Vimalakirti, the layman, like you and me, outdid all the Bodhisattvas Mahasattvas in answering the Buddha's question?

You mean when they all gave clever replies—and he kept silent?

Yes, Mañjusri nearly got it right, but he was unwise enough to say it. Like Mahakasyapa, in the Flower Sermon, Vimalakirti merely smiled—if he even did that.

Because it cannot be said? There can be no name for that "Who?"

You can give him a name as long as a Welsh railway-station if you like, that matters very little.

Then what does matter?

That there is no one and no thing to name.

So that what is speaking, answering, whatever it be, is just nothing?

No, not "nothing"—"nothing" is still some thing.

Then the absence of nothing?

Shen Hui might have passed that in China eleven hundred years ago but neither you nor I may do so to-day.

Why is that?

He knew better than we do, but perhaps our dialectics have gone deeper.

Even absence is some thing?

Is it not a concept like any other? Then who is conceiving?

I have it, I have it!

Good man!

But I cannot say it!

Still better man! Why?

Because . . . because . . . how shall I put it? What is conceiving cannot conceive what is conceiving, like an eye that cannot see what is looking? And that is "Who?"!

All "who"s, also "you" and "I"—and all "I"s.

Surely there is only one "I"?

One? One what, where, when? There is no "one" in the universe, no even one.

Just all do-ing, say-ing, think-ing, even be-ing. Shen Hui would have called that "Prajña." May we?

Yes, let's allow him to get away with that one! It's Sanscrit at least! But a Welsh railway-station will do just as well.

Consciousness cannot be conscious of consciousness, and therefore is unconscious and no "thing"? Has no subject?

Surely. Like a mirror, as Chuang Tzu said, reflects what is in front of it, makes no remarks about it, rude or polite, and keeps nothing.

He did not say that!

Perhaps, but he meant it. Anyhow, whoever said it, is it not evident? Consciousness, being-conscious, is unconscious of consciousness.

But who knows it as "consciousness"?

We do. It is a concept, totally imaginary, also called "mind."

And we are that?

It is no "that," you speak like a Vedantin, good as they are otherwise, but such is surely an image of what we are, all that we are, in so far as we can ever conceive it.

How do we know that?

Since you insist on a concept, is there anything else we could possibly resemble?

Then what is *one to make of this existing and non-existing business?*

Did not the Buddha have something to say on the subject?

I expect so. He generally did.

What was it? It has been widely publicised.

As far as I remember he is reputed to have said that it is all my eye.

Three letters, or one?

Three . . . e-y-e.

Copyist's error surely?

Perhaps! Would one letter have been better?

One letter is the only answer to any question.

In any case he was as solemn as ever!

Those who recorded what he had said, from three to nine centuries after his death, and in a couple of languages he never knew, certainly were, but one is at liberty to suspect him of a sense of humour in Maghadi!

Would we not have more confidence in him if he had cracked a few jokes?

Undoubtedly. To take *samsara* seriously, without the spice of humour, is owlish indeed.

Owls are reputed to see in the dark.

He saw further into the dark than either owls or men, so far that he saw right through into the light!

Is not the lack of humour in the sutras due to the religious wrappings in which they mummified his teaching nine and more generations after his parinirvana?

Religion can have that effect—even in the West. But we can believe what is attributed to him. He was usually right, whoever wrote his books and whenever they did it.

So it doesn't matter which kind of "eye" he was referring to?

How could it? Do you not understand the meaning of the famous statement that the Buddha spoke for fifty years, and no word ever passed his lips?

Yes, only split-mind speaks, and in Ch'an "the Buddha" means "Mind-only."

Such statements should be understood rather than explained.

Even between friends?

Many of our friends have four legs and explain nothing. Perhaps that is why they are so much more worthy of our friendship than we are of theirs?

And they do not know whether they exist or do not exist?

My guess is that they neither know nor care.

So it is unimportant to know whether we exist or do not exist?

What could it matter? Could you care less?

I could not. Unless knowing the answer had the effect of waking me up! Could it?

Any perception might have that effect, provided that you could take it and that it was not expected—that is if the Masters are to be believed. Which way would you like it anyhow—exist or not-exist or both or neither?

Which is the least somniferous? They all make me yawn!

And "neither . . . nor . . ." makes you snore?

Exactly, so what?

Do you really need my answer?

Yes, please: your answers nearly always manage to get by with me!

Thanks, old man! But that's a pity. And this one is so obvious that it really is not worth mentioning.

Never mind, let's have it.

Very well, then. No such question could possibly arise!

Why not?

Because it isn't a question at all.

Why is that?

Because it can have no answer. Where there is no answer how could there be a question?

Are there many such pseudo-questions?

As many as the other kind, but that is not commonly perceived.

I am not sure that I can see clearly just why this one is not a question.

I have already pointed that out to you, but you shied off it.

How?

I think I said a few minutes ago that it is because he does not exist—otherwise than as a *concept* in mind—that no man is able to *conceive* that he does not exist. Obvious now?

Not quite?

A concept cannot conceive its own conceptual inexistence.

At last! The question is not a question and need never have been asked.

And what a lot of harmless fun we should have missed!

Quite so. Better not to understand too much?

Some of the Masters held that view. There are other ways of approach—but surely *Jnana* is the greatest, the surest, and the most profound—though even that has to be voided in the end!

❧

Disputation and discussion are both futile.
Why is that?
Because nothing either party could say could possibly be true,
And whereas dispute picks out the false,
Which is too easy to see,
Discussion seeks the truth which is being pointed at,
Which is too difficult to describe.

64 – The Whole Story

I. The Insight

IT IS absolutely necessary to understand that there cannot *be* any such "thing" as an object, which is to say that an object is an appearance in mind and can have no other factual existence.

Nor, of course, can there *be* such a "thing" as *a* subject—since "such a thing" would then itself be an object, and so on *ad infinitum* in a perpetual regression.

It inevitably follows that the appearance of all that is objective is necessarily an objectivisation of whatever is perceiving it.

This will be found to be the perceiving itself, or the cognising, the "being aware of" or "being conscious of" whatever is cognised—and such can be termed THIS or I.

II. Comment

How can one apperceive that there cannot be such a "thing" as an object? The answer to that query has never been given, as far as I am aware, or the answers have been so long and elaborate that they have filled volumes and can hardly be termed answers to a specific query.

It just has to be apperceived—for it is an inseeing, quite obvious, inescapable, when present in consciousness, but laborious indeed when dialectically elaborated in the objective medium of language. For that process is itself incompatible with what it is seeking to establish, since an objective medium is engaged in proving the inexistence of what is then functioning.

Since the question "What is an object?" can have no

answer, dialectically-speaking, it cannot be a question at all, and objectivity must be taken as a "given" factor in phenomenal living, as it has always been taken as the basis of scientific experiment and of philosophical thought.

Metaphysics alone seeks to transcend conceptuality and such is the specific function of metaphysics. So-functioning, seeking dualistically to conceive non-conceptuality, it can only record inseeing symbolically or by indication. An object, therefore, can only be understood as an objecti*fication* of its subject—subject making an object of what it is—or as an objecti*visation*—subject perceiving what it is as an object, and it can have no other being whatever.

But to regard such "subject" as an entity would be making an object of it, which is nonsense, for then it becomes a concept. Therefore it can only be apperceived negatively, neither as cogniser nor as cognised, but inferentially as what we call cognis*ing*, the apparently functional aspect of what to a reasoning mind can only be regarded as non-being.

Only one further step remains, or is possible, and that is to apperceive that this which is inconceivable must be whatever is vainly seeking to conceive it, which is whatever is responsible for formulating these words and also whatever is concerned in understanding them. And for such uncognisable non-entity we have only one word in any language, which is the first person singular of the verb "to be," "I" apparently plural in functioning, theoretically singular, but which, metaphysically apprehended, must be as totally devoid of the one as it is of the other attribute.

Furthermore since an object, in order to be apparent, must be conceptually extended spatially and temporally, any being it could have must lie in its inherent subjectivity, much as that of a shadow must lie in its substance. Its subjectivity might perhaps be said to be both immanent and transcendent, but phenomenally the object can only be an appearance, as a shadow is, whereas noumenally it cannot be said to have any objective existence whatever.

We are conditioned to regard the phenomenal as existent, but in order to apprehend what we are such conditioning has to be discarded; what is sensorially perceived is then seen as the purely conceptual structure in mind which is all that it can be. Many of those who know this seek to regard the noumenal as existent (or "real" as they term it) instead, but clearly it is nothing of the kind. "Existence" as such is conceptual and cannot possibly be otherwise, and noumenality, not having any objective quality, cannot be conceived. Moreover noumenality is conceiving, and what is conceiving cannot conceive what is conceiving.

What is objectively extended in conceptual spacetime cannot be said to have other than conceptual and phenomenal existence, and its noumenon cannot be conceived at all, so that no concept such as that of "existence" can be applied to it.

That, we may presume, is what Hui Neng meant when he saw and stated that "from the beginning nothing exists."

"What you are looking for is what is looking."
(The unholy Wei Wu Wei? Actually—no:
attributed to the holy St. Francis of Assisi).

65 ·⁀ The Perfect Way

The Perfect Way knows no difficulties
Except that it refuses to make preferences.
The Hsin Hsin Ming (p. 219)

Why is "discrimination" or "preference" condemned by all the sages? Surely that is because it can only be possible to experience what we are?

We can experience positively or negatively, which are interdependent counterparts whose mutual contradiction renders experience agreeable or disagreeable and thereby requires a suppositional entity to suffer the experience.

"Preference" is preferring the agreeable to the disagreeable, and as long as that discrimination obtains there is apparent bondage to *samsara* which requires a space-time "entity" to suffer this experience of what it is.

But as long as we regard as "entities" what objectively we are we cannot avoid such discrimination. The idea of an entity endeavouring not to discriminate must be absurd, for it is the discriminating that requires the "entity," so that an entity can only cease to discriminate by ceasing to be an "entity." Then there will be no one to "discriminate," and that is precisely all that the sages recommended.

An entity that ceased to discriminate should thereby lose its "ens"—for discriminating is its *raison-d'être*—but by what power can it thus commit suicide—for suicide that would be? The apparent "power" or initiative of an entity can never be its own, since its purely conceptual existence cannot give it any power. Its apparent "power" is therefore derivative—an objective appearance like all that appertains to it.

It follows that the source of its apparent "power," as of all power, is not phenomenal but noumenal. It follows also that such power can never be exercised as an "act of will" by a phenomenal "identity," though it may be manifested by such, but must always be a direct or indirect manifestation of the immanent aspect of transcendence expressed in space-time.

Therefore, since the abolition of "discrimination" and "preference" can only occur via the abolition of a pseudo-entity to exercise them, such abolition can only supervene as a result of understanding that there can be no such "thing" as an "entity" in the universe, which implies that all phenomenality is conceptual, as are all dreams, ecstasies and psychic states whatsoever.

Then all that seems to remain is I, and I am no "thing" and therefore cannot "remain." I cannot "remain" since I have never either been or not-been, present or absent, conceptually; my presence is never absence nor my absence ever presence. So subsisting, no question such as "discrimination" or "preference" can arise.

Note: "Discrimination," "preference," etc, are colloquial terms used by translators for what more technically is just "conceptualising," These indefinite locutions have an affective implication which requires a volitional comparison between pairs of mutually contradictory concepts. But they have become doctrinal jargon and have lost any precision they ever had, So used to-day they tend to produce confusion and, ultimately, despair, whereas technical terms, correctly used, retain their validity and develop understanding.

Definition of all "others"
"There—but for the grace of God—go I."
My "self" and the beetle included? Why, of course!

66 · Non-Conceptually—What?

WHAT CAN be the significance of blessing and adoring a concept, let us say of a merciful and paternal deity as "God," or of cursing and loathing a concept of a merciless and inimical deity as "the Devil," since there is nothing for either to be but what we ourselves are who are doing it?

Unless we have perceived the obviously conceptual nature of every objectivisation in mind, we can never be free from our conceptual "bondage," since "bondage" is itself a concept dependent on the existence of a "universe" or "cosmos" which itself is entirely conceptual.

Until we have perceived that our whole "life," from "birth" to "death," inclusive, is entirely conceptual, and that we can know nothing whatever that is other than conceptual, including the conceptual "we" who appear to be conceiving it all, we surely cannot expect to apperceive the *source* of all this vast structure of objectivisation. And this is, clearly must be, what we are other than the objective plurality of apparent "beings" which we have been misconditioned to suppose that we are.

This is the clearance which is all that "split" or relative mind can achieve in order to bring us face-to-face with what we are, and which is done by bringing us face-to-face with what we cannot be and are not except as conceptual objects.

Having understood by relative reasoning that whatever is conceptual is precisely a space-time image objectivised in mind appearing to exist as a phenomenal "presence," we are left so-to-speak with our non-objective "nature" which hitherto has been a noumenal "absence"—and such is Suchness, Buddha-mind, Bhutatathata, Tao, the Kingdom of Heaven, Nirvana, or whatever fancy conceptual name we have been using in our necessarily futile endeavours to conceptualise what we are.

Yet, if we care to say—each and all of us—that what we are is I conceptually identified with objects cognised as "me" and "you," are we not expressing this understanding as accurately as it could ever be indicated in any relative language of our objectifying or "split" mind? No doubt, but if in so-doing we are still conceptualising the personal pronoun "I" as any "thing" whatsoever—then we are merely rattling the conceptual chains with which we think we are bound.

As the source of the three dimensions of conceptual "space," extended in which all objects appear, and of the fourth conceptualised as "duration," in which all objects appear to "last" so that their appearance may be cognisable, what we are as this noumenal source of cognition can never be cognised by any means or in any guise whatsoever, since it is what we are who are cognising.

Note: Since the ideas of "existing" or "being" are themselves conceptual it follows inevitably that what we are cannot either "exist" or "be," "not-exist," or "not-be," i.e. "exist" or "be" either positively or negatively, for these are notions, figments of imagination, like all the others. That is why, when we seek to perceive what we are, what is then not perceived is called "Void" which again is only a concept in mind.

If you, as "I," were to say "Me-less, I neither am nor am-not," and clearly insee it, should that not be turning the conceptualising faculty back upon itself, and should it not then be pointing negatively at what it is nonconceptually? Conceptually, never can I "be," but here is not conceptuality transcending itself by sheer negation? If this were so—"mind" should then be no longer "split" but "whole."

This would seem to be an example of the process of "retroversion" so lauded by the Bodhisattvas and accepted by the Buddha as the direct "way" of recognising the eternal "enlightened" state of all sentient-beings. Any of the sense-perceptions suffice, for whichever be used all conform instantaneously; in this case the sixth is in question.

67 ⁓ *Anecdote*

Consciousness is never experienced in the plural, only in the singular.

ERWIN SCHRÖDINGER

I had a terrible experience this morning. I do not often go into the town, but for once I did.

Everywhere I looked I saw people carrying a signboard on which was written the words "I exist"—and on many the words "And How" were added. All except young children, cats and dogs.

It was horrifying! But, I said to myself, you are all my objects, all objects in my mind! Don't you know that? How, then, can you imagine that you exist as your*selves?*

Poor deluded people, weighed down by a terrible illusion, all lost, all miserable—for *what an appalling burden to have to bear!*

I turned round to go home, my heart heavy with compassion. Just think—unremitting responsibility for every apparent action, past, present, and future! *Ecrasant!!*

On the way home I passed another man; this one, perhaps a psychic who caught my thought, saw me and murmured "Quite so, you also, poor old chap!"

So we all suffer from the same delusion! And suffer indeed we do—as the Buddha observed.

Whatever for?

No good blaming them for making an object of *me:* each of us is making an object of himself too!

Only bodhisattvas and buddhas don't do it?

And that is why they are bodhisattvas and buddhas?

So they don't "suffer." And nobody "suffers" since their not-suffering abolishes all suffering?

Why so? Because there is nobody else to suffer—or to be anybody else.

How obvious, how simple; only needs noticing!

Noticing? Precisely—but a rather special kind of noticing:

The kind wherein there is nobody to notice that there is nothing to be noticed.

68 ∙ Not for a Moment

NOT FOR a moment, a split-second of temporality, a *ksana,* could any object exist apart from its subject (or any subject apart from its object). Even in the sequence of time never are they two otherwise than as concepts, and apart from the sequence of time they are not concepts.

"Non-objective relation" is precisely this identity of subject and object recognised as mutual, and implies This-which-I-am.

This identity applies also to Noumenon and its phenomena, which never can be apart—again even in temporality, for Intemporality and time are inseparable also.

Noumenon is immanent in all its phenomena, which it transcends, and Transcendence is inseparable from immanence (which is phenomenal).

This-which-I-am, therefore, transcending-that-which-I-appear-to-be, is immanent therein, and never in a temporal context can they be two, except as concepts.

In every moment of an apparent "life" in duration, noumenally I-AM and phenomenally I-am-not as an object, which is a concept in mind. Therefore, whereas phenomenally as a conceptual object I neither am nor am not, noumenally never for a moment do I cease to be I (This-which-I-am).

If we can inhere in this indefectable identity, which is our totality, and which phenomenally is a conceptual objectivisation, there remains no basis for the incongruous notion that what each of us is could be an autonomous phenomenon, an objectivised conceptual appearance in mind.

Our phenomenal limitation is illusory as limitation, but our phenomenality is not illusory as such, for it is inherent in our noumenality, whose expression it is, and which is all that it is.

Therein the burden of imaginary bondage can have no place—for what we are transcends conceptual space-time on which all sentience depends for its extension in manifestation.

69 ⁓ Not Even Absolute

I

IT COULD not make the slightest difference metaphysically whether "you" or "I" are conceived as "absent" or "present." As long as "a you" or "an I" is conceived as being "there" or "here" to be either "absent" or "present," the situation remains unchanged.

Nor could it matter how far "back" we might go in negation or self-naughting: as long as there is a *negator* to negate "we" still remain un-negated.

Such is the problem—and apparently insoluble. And that is why "we" cannot solve it, nor ever shall be able to solve it.

For the same reason as that whereby there can be no difference between object and subject there can be no difference between negation and affirmation. Nor can there be any difference between the opposing elements of any pair of interdependent counterparts, for in relativity there will always be a conceptual entity to which they are being applied, whereas Absolutely none such can be conceived.

Thereby we can understand that "difference" as such is *relative* to a differentiator, whereas *absolutely* there could not be any such conceptual entity, so that "no" and "yes" become identical. Should not this understanding throw open the prison of dualist phenomenality wherein we are apparently confined, thereby revealing our unique non-unicity?

II

Why should this be so? Because non-phenomenally there could not be any difference, "difference" being conceptual, and non-conceptual noumenality—which is therefore inconceivable—can only be a symbol for whatever we must be.

"Noumenality," however, is an ambiguous symbol, for the term is applicable to the counterpart of "phenomenality"—*which latter is what we are objectively*—and what is in question cannot adequately be represented by a relative symbol.

"Noumenality," therefore, only goes as far as relative reasoning can take us. It may be regarded as pointing to its own transcendence and to that of its counterpart "phenomenality," and such absolute transcendence, as which we neither are nor are not, may less unhappily be recorded by the three letters T A O.

III

It is evident that there cannot be anyone (any factual entity) to experience either element of any pair of interdependent counterparts, so that neither affirmation nor negation of either element can factually apply, for all are just concepts in mind.

Whose concepts? And in what "mind"? Nobody's concepts, concepts of experiencing as such. So what is experiencing? Relatively, nothing factual is experiencing, for "experiencing" is conceptual, and absolutely there can not be any "thing" to experience or to be experienced. "Experiencing," therefore, is the "mind" that experiences "experience."

Moreover experience is extended in space-time, and can only appear to occur dualistically as a phenomenon. Therefore what noumenally it is can only be whatever we are who appear to experience it.

Experienced, "experience" (experiencing mind) is relative; unexperienced, "experience" (experiencing mind) must be absolute: in either case—manifested or unmanifest—"it" represents what we are, and as such we are not any entity which could be either affirmed or negated.

For then we are beyond relativity, beyond divided experiencing mind, beyond affirmation and negation, so that nothing whatever can either be affirmed or negated concerning what *absolutely* we are.

If we can in-see this, which is in-seeing what is inseeing, there cannot be anything to "see" or to be "seen," but then what is in-seeing must necessarily be what can most simply be recorded as

Note: "We" cannot take refuge even in the Absolute, for "the Absolute" is also our image and so our object. But the Absolute must be what-I-am, both subjectively and objectively, and every sentient-being can be aware of it.

70 ·- Lachez-Prise!—A Dialogue

Why are you looking at me like that?

I am not looking at you: I am looking at myself.

How so?

All that I see is my object, and my object is my self manifesting.

Then what about *my* self?

Your self is always my self, whoever says it.

How many selves are there?

None as such; one—phenomenally regarded—as subject of phenomenal objects.

Then what I am to you is what you are to me?

Precisely.

So that phenomenally I am both self and other?

And noumenally I am neither.

Looking at objects is looking at what-I-am in manifestation?

There can be no other means of observing what you are.

And the more profoundly I look the more fully I see what

I am?

What you are, objectivised, of course.

And I have no other means of knowing what I am?

None whatever.

So that all relation is ultimately non-objective?

Which is no-relation.

Then really there is no such "thing" as an object?

"Really"—there could not be: an object is only its subject manifesting.

Then there are two degrees of manifestation?

If you wish: noumenal subject—which has, of course, no phenomenal existence—manifesting phenomenally by means of the mechanism of duality.

Which is? . . .

A suppositional subject perceiving an apparent object, and such object apparently perceiving other objects.

The two degrees are really one?

Not even one: "degrees" are subject to the phenomenon of duration. Manifestation occurs in a time-sequence, in which a supposed subject perceives a supposed object. But nothing has happened noumenally.

So that there is no difference between observer and observed?

How could there be? What is perceived is a space-time mirage—like any dream or hallucination.

But can I find myself by regarding myself as an object?

Surely not! You have never lost yourself, and there is no "thing" to find.

You are evading my question! If I profoundly examine an object I am profoundly examining my *self.*

You, as I, are empirically examining a dualised expression of what I am, by means of split-mind. There is no thing to find, and no one to find anything.

But can it not lead me back to what I am?

You cannot be led back to what you are, to what I am, but awareness of the obvious might supervene.

But, though I know that, I am not aware of it in the sense of living it.

Of course you are, though you may not perceive it.

But I am not *profoundly* aware of it!

You are *profoundly aware of it; it is superficially, via your split-mind, that you think you are not.*

But I want to awaken to that awareness.

Sleepers do not awaken themselves by an act of volition.

Then what awakens them?

I only observe that it happens when it is due to happen.

And I can do nothing to make it happen?

Most certainly not! Whatever "you" try to do will prevent it happening.

So what?

So what? There must neither be a do-ing nor a not-doing—in order to allow *it to* happen.

❧

Absence of an entity to be enlightened
Or not to be enlightened
Is the double negative, the double absence,
Of Shen Hui and all the Great Masters.

71 ∙ The Mirage—A Trilogy

I. ONE AND ALLNESS
II. THE FIRST PERSON SINGULAR
III. THE DOOR IS OPEN—A DIALOGUE

I. One and Allness

The expression "disidentification," as a more accurate definition of what is inferred by the term "enlightenment," or "awakening" thereto, is far indeed from being satisfactory.

"Disidentification" requires "identification"—the identification of A with B, of one objective entity with another objective entity. It also implies the possibility of the "reidentification" of one object with another object. Whereas what is necessary should imply the total abolition of any kind of entification whatever.

The apparent situation, which is associated with the phenomenal condition called "bondage," is the functioning in a space-time context of split-mind, whereby the conceptual subject regards what it is as an object. "It" does this because everything it perceives appears as an object, including what it regards as what is perceiving, what other phenomenal objects call by "its" name and perceive, which it also partially perceives physically and assumes to be "itself." A pardonable error surely? Pardonable and universal.

But the understanding that this is not so, that "perceiving," like all forms of sentience, is a space-time objectivisation or manifestation of an undivided and indivisable condition of "being conscious," should be capable of disposing of this error, of this entifying of a concept of split-mind. No doubt, if we were not so profoundly conditioned by upbringing, "education," and environmental influence, it should be. At least it is not difficult to apprehend, so why should it be so difficult to apply?

The multiplication of objects produced by the splitting of "mind" into subject and its objects does not necessarily imply the multiplying of consciousness as such. That is a crude and ingenuous supposition, pardonable perhaps, but totally inacceptable to developed intelligence as also to noumenal inseeing.

The rectification of this error, the results of which are almost incredibly disastrous in phenomenal "living," is easy enough to comprehend. Thereby the entification of phenomenal subject must disappear: subject, even regarded as singular, is apperceived as noumenon, and all that is sensorially perceptible is apperceived as phenomena. Then everything becomes an object in "mind" or "consciousness," and no subjective element remains phenomenally at all.

Apparent subjectivity is thus seen as second-degree or reflected subjectivity, somewhat like one source of light reflected in a thousand mirrors, infinitely varied in reception, according to the form and situation of the mirror in space-time, but all being diversified reflections of the single source.

This, of course, is only a provisional picture, still a dualistic interpretation of split-mind, but in this imperfect manner we can all apprehend it. Metaphysically "mind" or "consciousness" is neither more nor less singular than it is plural, both of which are entirely conceptual, as is "mind" itself. What is referred to as "whole-mind" or "consciousness" is a concept also, but it can be a symbol for what we are, which is all we possibly could be, or "I."

As such it can have no objective quality whatever, which means that what it is can not have any phenomenal existence. This means that what it is cannot be conceived objectively and so cannot be any thing we can know—since we are not able to know anything that cannot be objectified. Nor is it only a question of dualised intellectual knowledge, it cannot be recorded by any kind of sense-perception either—since it is the subjective being of what all these are, and no objective phenomenon can know its own noumenon which is all that it can be.

Therefore what we are cannot be thought or said to exist at all, in any sense or manner in which that concept can be understood by split-mind. Nor can it be conceived by whatever "whole-mind" may be or may not be, for "whole-mind" is no objective "thing," nor does it conceive.

To us this may present itself as an insoluble mystery, but there need not be anything "mysterious" about it at all, for "mystery" is just another concept in split-mind. To an accomplished "Sage" it does not appear as a "mystery," for he is what it is—as we are. He is integrated with what he is—with what we are, and as a "man of Tao" who is Tao and knows it.

But being what it is, as it is what he is, he can know no more *about* it than can you or I, since there cannot be any "entity" to know or to be known.

II. The First Person Singular

Identification being the identifying of one object with another, in order that identification can occur at all it is necessary that I become an object which shall be identified with a phenomenon which then will be known as "I": Nominative-I become accusative-"I" (*moi* in French). This analytical statement should perhaps reveal the artifice whereby this false dialectical process has become acceptable.

I could never in any circumstance be or become an object; such an arbitrary transformation is a contradiction-in-terms. It follows that so thinking is false thinking, dialectically inadmissible. *I* must always be subject, subject of all objects cognised. I can never in any circumstance be an object of what *I* am, and this applies to whoever says "I."

Therefore dialectically I am always singular, a singular that can never have plurality. The accusative of "I" is "you," can only be "you," for "me" would be a *non-sequitur,* self-contradictory and meaningless; as subject "you" are always I, as object I am always "you."*

In fact here we only need to think and speak rationally in order to be in accordance with metaphysical truth. And the metaphysical truth is simply that I, subjectively, am devoid of plurality, and appear as "singular" only when regarded as a concept.

The ultimate understanding, therefore, can be expressed by the statement that I cannot *do* anything whatever—for the evident reason that *there is no I* to DO anything whatever.

This does not imply that nothing can appear to be done: indeed the apparent universe is dependent on "action." But such action is known as *yu wei,* like the apparent writing of these lines. These lines appear to have been written, but no "I" wrote them, which is why they are attributed to *wu wei.* This is why the Chinese masters could say that the Buddha preached for 49 years but no word passed his lips, and that a man could walk for a thousand *li* but did not take a step outside his own house; and many other variations on the same theme.

The essential understanding is incompatible with entification, and any supposed form of release from "bondage" that leaves an "entity" experiencing it, however enjoyable that experience may be, is not release from bondage at all—for bondage and entification are one and the same phenomenon.

---

* When a child says "Give Tommy a sweet," not "Give I, or me, a sweet," he has not yet been conditioned to the basic error—the objective personification of what he is as I.

III. The Door Is Open—A Dialogue

1

I am *not* nothing!

Why so?

Because I am *not* anything to be nothing.

You mean? . . .

I would have to be something in order to be nothing, but I am not any thing.

Why?

In order to *be* nothing I would have to *be.* I have to be in order even to say that I am not.

Since you cannot say that you are nothing, it cannot be true?

It cannot. But I can truly say that I am not any thing. I can say that what I am is not anything that objectively appears, nor anything that can be imagined, visualised, sensorially perceived, or cognised.

2

Can I say that I do not exist? I can only insist that I have no objective existence that is other than apparent, which appearance is conceptual and so does not establish existence as such.

Can you say that you do not exist as "I," or that you are not as "I"?

If "existence" and "being" imply objectivity as "I," I certainly can say it. But if not—that cannot be said either.

Nevertheless it can be known, whatever the implication of the words?

Since "existence" and "being" must necessarily imply objectivity, and any other sense is inacceptable, it can be regarded as the ultimate, total, and absolute truth, in so far as "truth" can ever be said to be true.

Is there no way of saying it without the possibility of misinterpretation?

There is: a further degree of negation.

Which is?...

I neither exist nor do not exist, I neither am nor am not.

Which mean?...

What I am is inexpressible by means of any concept such as "existence" or "being"—nor is what I am conceptually definable at all.

So that?...

Any attempt whatever to express or to apprehend what I am—which is what you are—is closing an open door in order to pass through it.

72 ·– *The Mechanism of Relativity*

RELATIVITY, OR reasoning by means of the comparison of opposing concepts, is necessarily a psychological process which is only applicable to the description of objects.

Its operation psychically creates such objects as images in mind, in order to compare them with other objects, and it likewise imagines qualities to be compared with opposing qualities that are to be attributed to the object being described.

Since the objects so conceived require a subject in order that they may appear as objects the process of conceiving is then itself conceived as the conceiver.

This is a brief indication of how duality arises and of the emergence of an I-concept or "ego."

In this process what is conceiving could never by any means be conceived, since what is conceiving cannot be an object and so cannot be conceived by "itself." It follows that whatever may be the degree of efficacy of relative thought in the accurate description of objects, it can have no degree whatever of efficacy in describing whatever is not objective. This implies that such efficacy as it may have for physical and philosophical reasoning is automatically inoperative when it is employed for reasoning about whatever is metaphysical. Relative reasoning can have nothing to offer whenever it is applied to the subjective and the noumenal.

It should be sufficiently clear that the reason for this is the presence of the suppositional subject which is brought into *theoretical* existence in order to account for the *apparent* existence of objects as phenomena in mind.

Is it not clear also that none of this can have any but a conceptual existence in mind, and that the source of this psychic construction is the conceiving as such—about which nothing whatever could possibly be conceived?

Surely it follows that whatever relative thinking may have to say about noumenality must necessarily be nonsense, and that whatever understanding of noumenality may be possible can only be obtained directly, by mentation that is not relative, that is not objectivising, that is not employing the process of conceptualisation by means of the comparison of opposing concepts?

For this reason, which itself is relative conceptualising, noumenality cannot be objectivised by any means whatever, which is to say that it may be apprehended but that it can never be conceptualised or expressed accurately in any form of words. Therefore to argue about it must necessarily be futile, for its apprehension belongs to a non-relative in-seeing that can not be either present or absent in a time-context, but which is the integrality of mind, undivided into a suppositional subject and its objects.

Does this sufficiently explain why it is axiomatic in metaphysics that there is no do-er nor anything done, but only a do-*ing* which is the conceiv-*ing* of whatever action may appear to be performed?

Note: Relativity, or divided-mind, is whole-mind *split by conceptualising.* It is "mind" conceptually dividing into apparent object and the suppositional subject of that object.

Did you see that?
Yes, of course.

Well, do you believe it?
Why do you ask?
Because for you seeing-is-believing,
For me seeing is—just *seeing*

73 ~ Quips and Queries - IV

Understanding cannot be reached by reasoning,
And things are only a reflection in Mind.

It is not sufficient to eschew practice: it is necessary also to eschew non-practice. Both forms of practice are incompatible with liberation, for liberation means liberation from a practiser.

All positivity is illusory,
Only in the negation of the positive (that which is objectivised) can we know what we are.

There is no causality in dreams,
That is why they are called inconsequent.

❧

Whoever thinks that he exists objectively is like a dog barking up a tree that isn't there.

"Truth" is always relative
(and therefore cannot be *true*).

The "Positive Way" is not a way:
It is a dead end.

Phenomenally we are inferential entities whose *bona fides* will not stand examination.

PART V

Absence

Noumenally I am transcendence,
Phenomenally I am immanence,
And all-that-is I am.

74 ·- The Question and the Answer

I am the answer, what is being looked-for, the sought, and as such unfindable.

Precisely because it is I that am ask*ing*, look*ing*, or seek*ing*, and so am devoid of objective or apparent being.

For I am neither object nor subject, but the presence of the mutual absence of both—which is the only presence there could ever be.

Why is this so? Because all things appear extended in space-time, and their extension, and all that is extended, is what I am.

Note: Yes, you can say it also, and any apparent sentient being.

We are conditioned to suppose that what we are is the presence of what is present, which is the absence of what is absent.

But when we apperceive what we are we find that what we are is the absence of what is present, and presence of what is absent.

75 ·- Singular Saying

I

I am singular,
And whatever appears to be done
I "do" it.

If you should imagine that "you" do it
"You" are mistaken,
For there is no "you,"
And I am not plural.

Every apparent sentient-being can say "I,"
For *I* am all that he is.
Some sentient-beings cannot speak?
Their function-*ing* is their speech,
And their every movement says "I."

II

Your trouble, sometimes called "bondage,"
Is that "you" try to "do" things,
Which is a work of supererogation,
And "you" tend to attribute what I do
To "yourself."

That, however, is a myth,
A phantasy or a dream.
Let Me say "I"—and you are free.

III

I am forever I,
Noumenally and phenomenally,
Here and Now, always and everywhere,
And whoever says it.

Timeless and infinite,
There is no "other,"
Nor any "one."

❧

I am the light that falls on ten thousand specks of dust so that each may shine.

76 ·- Lux in Tenebris

I, who am Light, cannot know darkness.
Wherever I look throughout the extension of space,
Wherever my glance falls
Along the long line of extended time,
Nowhere is darkness to be found.

What, then, is this objective dream,
Darkened by objects, objects which "suffer"?
Where can I find them, what can they be
But the shining of the Light which I am?

My shining is necessarily their being;
As "specks of dust" they are darkness unseen,
As I am unseen Light wherever they are not.
Only when my radiance falls upon them do they appear,
Only when I touch them do *I* shine.

Noumenally, I who am Light
Phenomenally appear as darkness.
Objectively, they who are darkness
Subjectively appear as Light—when I shine.
Where I am, darkness cannot be,
For in my Presence darkness can only be Light.

Objects are nought but my shining;
Their colours are the refraction of my Light,
For without me they cannot appear,
And without them I cannot be known.

Nor is there "space" save when I shine,
Nor "time" which is the measure of my shining.
My shining is the appearance of objects,
And shining is my appearance as Light.

77 ·-- Practice of Non-Practice

WHENEVER YOU are absent as "you," You are present as I. So you may say "My absence as 'me' is My presence as I."

Of course I am always present as I, but when I *appear* to be present as "you" (or as "me") I seem to be absent, i.e. My presence appears to be an absence.

Also you may say "My absence as 'that' (which can be known) is My presence as THIS" (about which there cannot be anything to know).

If one were to think it, apperceive it, understand it, even occasionally? . . .

Note: When I am present as "you" I seem to last, to be extended in "time." When I am present as "you" others think they see me as "you," and they see a few bits of "your" surfaces, and other bits reflected in mirrors, but only bits and all surfaces, so that I appear as "form," extended in "space."

When I am present as I, I have no objective appearance at all to need extension, and I am no "thing" to have "duration." It is only as "you" that I am extended in form as appearance and require duration as time. As "me" I am not at all, for when I am objectified I am always "you" since all form soever is My "you."

I can only be seen or known as "you," but there are no "others" at all—only "you" as I, for except as appearance I *am* not in any sense "you" could understand—since "you" can only understand what "you" can objectify in "your" split-minded condition, and "you" cannot objectify what I am because I am all that "you" are.

78 ·- Reminder

Whatever may be speaking as "I"
Is always speaking from HERE.
It may be a relative "I,"
Or I may be speaking directly.

Whatever relatively I may say
May seem to be a travesty of the truth,
May seem unworthy, contestable, or untrue,
But it is I who say it.

Whatever you may be hearing as "you,"
Always seems to be heard from THERE.
It may be a relative "you" that is hearing,
Or I may be hearing directly.

Whatever relatively "you" may hear,
May seem to be a mockery of what "you" believe,
May seem stupid, meaningless, or false,
But it is I who hear it.

I AND YOU

Absent, I apperceive,
Absent, I apprehend,

Absent, I act.

Present, you conceptualise,
Present, you judge,
Present, you react.

Absent, I rejoice,
Present, you suffer,
Absent, I am,
Present, you are not.

79 ·- As the Owl Remarked to the Rabbit

I am not subject to space, therefore I know no "where,"
I am not subject to time, therefore I know no "when,"
What space-time is I am, and nothing finite appertains to me.
Being nowhere I am every "where," being everywhere I am no "where,"
For I am neither any "where" nor no "where,"
Neither inside nor outside any thing or no thing,
Neither above nor below, before nor after, at either side of any or no thing.
I do not belong to that which is perceptible or knowable,
Since perceiving and knowing is what I am,
I am not *beyond* hither or thither, within or without,
Because they too are what I am.
I am not extended in space, I am not developed in duration;
All these are my manifestations, all these are conceptual images of what I am,
For it is my absence, my absolute absence, that renders

concepts conceivable.
I am ubiquitous, both as absence and as presence,
Since, as I,
I am neither present nor absent.
I can never be known as an object in mind,
For I am what is knowing, and even "mind" is my object.
"Quite so, I will digest it," replied the rabbit, but it was "he" who was digested.

80 ·- *You and I*

I HAVE NO apparent existence as I, as I (Self) I cannot appear: my appearance is "you" ("other").

Why cannot I appear as I?
Because I cannot conceive conceiving—which I am as I.
When conceiving conceives, what is conceived thereby appears as other-than-conceiving—since it is conceiving extended in space-time.
Therefore every object that is conceived appears as other-than-I.
The whole conceptual universe appears as other than-I,
But it is still I—for what else could there be for it to be?
All appearance is my appearance—self appearing as other.
Appearances—you, me, it, him, her, us, them, that, those, are I as other-than-I, "self" conceived as "other."
But they *are* not, they do not exist, as any thing but conceptual appearances in mind,
And I am not as any thing whatsoever—since I cannot be conceived at all.

That is what "things" are in so far as suchness may be expressed in the relative language of divided mind, of mind conceptually split into subject and object.

You may think that your whole problem is re-cognising yourselves as what you are, as what you have never ceased to be, and apart from which you are only appearances in mind, in "mind" which is also a concept and has no existence except as I?

But you have no power to cognise what you are, or to re-cognise it, or to cognise at all—for all that you are is I.

I need no cognising. You have only to abandon the illusory concept of being "you"—some thing, some object, *the practice of trying to conceive yourself at all*—since, as I, you cannot.

Unconceived as an appearance in mind, you have never been anything else, any "other," but always I—for space-time, in which your appearance appears, is conceptually imagined whenever conceiving conceives.

All the great Masters have told us this, each in his own way, that you are I—for there is no objectified appearance that could be anything else.

Memorable
That entire conceptual universe
Is *this* consciousness Which I am,
I who am not.

81 ~ *Hence the Universe*

I am: you appear,
I look: you see,

I listen: you hear,
I touch: you feel,
I act: you move,
I apperceive: you perceive,
I apprehend: you know.

Then you say
"I am, I see, I hear,
I feel, move, perceive and know,"
But you are wrong:
Mistaken identity
And bondage!*

Disciples—Devotees—Idolaters
What are most of them doing?
Worshipping the tea-pot
Instead of drinking the tea!

82 ·- I Looking

I, negative, thereby am negating positive,
I, positive, thereby am negating negative,
Withdrawn from conceiving,
I, neither negative nor positive,
Am then the negation of both concepts.

* For you also are I, of course.

But there were never either two "I"s
Or one, for such have only a conceptual existence.

❧

I am everything
Because no-thing is what I am.

83 ∽ The Unmanifest

I am the hearing of whatever is heard,
The seeing of whatever is seen,
The feeling and knowing of whatever is felt and known,
For I am the dreaming of whatever is dreamed,
And there is no I but the dreaming,
For the "I," in my dreaming is dreamed also.

The sense-perceptions and the cognising of them comprise all that there can seem to be phenomenally, and their perceivers and cognisers are conceptual also.

The painter is not in the picture, nor the dreamer in the dream, and they too are just concepts. I am the painting, the dreaming, the forever unmanifest source of all that is manifest, manifest only as all manifestation.

I am the source of what is experienced, but I do not suffer experience—for what suffers experience is an objectivisation of what I am. Only an object is real (a thing) and can suffer experience; *phenomenally* I am only a shadow, all shadows, and shadows do not suffer the experiences of their material substance. *Phenomenally* I am a reflection, and reflections do not suffer the experiences of their objects. *Phenomenally* regarded *you* are the substance, and I am the shadow. And it is phenomenally that you regard.

But *noumenally* I am the Sun, the source of light, whereby substance appears by objective resistance to my light, and I cast your shadow wherever you may turn.

Note: Not the way round you usually visualise it? Is it any the less pertinent for that?

84 ·- Transcendence and Immanence

I am not in front of you, I am not behind you,
Nor am I outside, or inside,
I am not above, nor am I below.

I am neither here nor there,
Neither near or far,
I am not anywhere, nor am I nowhere.

For where could there be any "where"
Wherein I could be?

I have never come nor shall I ever go,
I know no before, nor any after,
I am not old, and I was never young.

For whenever could there be a "when?"
During which I could be?

I am not any thing, nor no thing,
For what thing could there be
That I could be, or not be,
Since there is no "I"?

Note: It is interesting to remember that when Sri Ramana Maharshi was dying, he asked why people were weeping and was told that it was because he was leaving them. He answered, in apparent surprise, "But where do they think I could go to?" Is there record of a greater "last word"? It would seem that its supreme significance is not yet very generally understood. But to "explain" it would reduce its stupendous import.

85 ·- Incidentally

I am awareness of all that is aware.

I am the seeing of whatever is being seen,
The hearing of whatever is being heard,
The perceiving of whatever is being perceived,
The knowing of whatever can be known,
The doing of whatever can appear to be done.

For I am awareness of everything whatsoever
Of which any sentient being can be aware.

And beyond awareness no thing is,
For no thing can be anything but awareness,
And there has never been anything that existed
Otherwise than as its awareness.

This is the whole truth
And every sentient being can be aware of it,
For "being aware" is all, absolutely all
That he is as a sentient being.

This simple and unstudied statement is a commonplace

expression of what all of us must know in our hearts, in the silence of a fasting mind, which represents what we think of as "humility" or the absence of conceptual I-ness, whereby each of us is free to apperceive what he is.

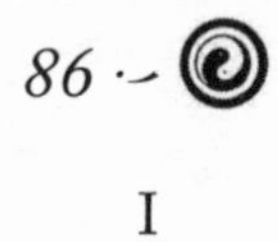

I

I am sensorially imperceptible,
Invisible, inaudible, invulnerable,
And incognisable.
That which can be perceived and cognized
Is relative,
Relatively, I am Absolute.

II

Relative phenomena,
Conceptualised as "me,"
Assuming subjective identity as "I,"
Perceive and cognise appearances as "other."

But there is no "me,"
There is no "other,"
For there is no "I."

No thing, I am all,
All, I am no thing.
Which is TAO.

III

Whatever is perceived by a "me,"
Conceived as "beautiful" or "ugly,"
I am its apperceiving.

Whatever is known by a "me,"
Conceived as "right" or "wrong,"
I am its apprehending.

Whatever is performed by a "me,"
Conceived as "good" or "evil,"
I am the doing of what is "done."

Whatever is suffered by a "me,"
Conceived as "pleasure" or "pain,"
I am the experiencing of its "experience."

And every sentient being says "me,"
For every sentient being is I.

IV

Every sentient being as such
Is relative and phenomenal,
Noumenally I am neither "relative" nor "absolute."

Every sentient being is a conceptual appearance
In divided "mind,"
And I am unperceivable
For I am neither "divided" nor "whole."

Every sentient being is extended in space-time,

And I am neither "finite" nor "infinite,"
Neither "temporal" nor "intemporal."

Every sentient being is either "present" or "absent,"
And I am neither "present" nor "absent,"
For I am the conceiving of conceiving,
Which is called TAO.

V

Absolute phenomenal absence
Is absolute noumenal presence.

Therefore Absolute absence is Absolute Presence.
Being absolute, how could they differ?

Which is TAO.

VI

I cannot know Myself as I,
But I can be Myself as I.
Why?
Because I am Myself as I.

Then there is no "self" to know,
Nor any "self" to be,
And I am all and no thing.

I can only be conceived as Awareness
Unaware of being aware,
Which is TAO.

Note: I am represented conceptually by "sentience" or "sentient consciousness."

87 ·- I, Functioning, See

There is no "I" here seeing any chair there;

There is no chair there being seen by any "I" here;

There is a seeing (appearing) of a chair-object, and a corresponding assumption of an I-subject—both chair-object and assumed I-subject being concepts in mind.

The seeing, however, as a phenomenon is not separate from its noumenon, for—as function-*ing*—it is an aspect of potential:

So I, functioning, see.

This applies to all sentient faculties.

All functioning occurs consecutively in time;

All functioning, therefore, produces concepts—imagery in mind.

All functioning is a temporal expression or manifestation of intemporality—intemporality manifesting as time.

Functioning, therefore, is inevitably and always I-functioning.

But such functioning is *wu wei, wu hsin, wu nien,* "direct," non-volitional functioning, unsubjected to dualistic subject/object interpretation by a conceptual autonomous "individual" appearing in temporality.

So-interpreted, what is seen—or otherwise sensorially conceived—has been termed "name and form" and is a dead concept, identified, filed, and embalmed in memory: it does not exist and has never existed. It is *sunyata* or "emptiness," void of being.

Such is phenomenal living, appearance, causation, *maya,* or the dream-phantasy of "existence."

Uninterpreted, such perception is I apperceiving an objectivisation of what I am—or noumenal living.

88 ·- No Other Teaching

NEED THERE be any other teaching, or any other understanding than the obvious—that what I-Here-Now AM is no object?

If I am no objective "thing" I am not a subject either, for "a subject" is an object.

Anything else but this direct understanding implies an entity having "views"—conceptualising.

Even this *can* be conceptual. If it be so, then I become some objectivised "thing." But I can not be thought—for what I am is necessarily unconscious of being conscious.

As a thought, conceptualised, I see what I am as that kind of object which is no-object. But what I am is not *"a"* no-object. I am total objective absence—which is total subjective presence, unaware of absence as of presence.

I, therefore, am NOT, wherefore I AM, I—who am necessarily every and no thing, and neither any nor no thing.

❧

All conceptualising is objectifying subject, a temporal process whereby subject seeks to objectify itself. For all knowledge is self-knowledge.

Note: Phenomenally regarded, "I" become an object of knowledge,

Noumenally regarded, I cannot be known at all.

As Noumenon, I unconsciously am.

Absolute is phenomenally negative, objects phenomenally positive. That is why only by totally negating the positive can Absolute be revealed, for the negation of phenomena lays bare Noumenon.

89 ⁓ Quips and Queries - V

The present absence, which is what I am, is the absent presence of my appearance.

Provided "you" don't interfere, you will find that you are I. Then whatever you may do, or not do, it is I who will do it, or not do it, for *there is no "you."*

For personal use

I am what remains when the last thing, the ultimate object, is denied.

My absence as a conceptual object is my presence as inconceivable subject.

Can I know darkness, I who am light?
Can I be absent—I who am *presence?*

Relatively regarded, every sentient being must be an incarnation of God.

Absolutely, every sentient being can only be whatever God is.

Losing oneself in what is Here
Is finding that "Here" is what one IS.

PART VI

Whole-Mind

When the ultimate object has been negated,
Then what remains is I,
And I am the affirmation of all that has been denied.

90 ·- The Beginning and the End

ANYONE THINKING, as an entity, about himself, as an entity, which entity has no existence other than as a concept in "his" mind, is wasting "his" time no matter what "he" may do. He is still a supposed subject regarding himself as a supposed object—and is not whole.

"Majesty," said Bodhidharma to the Emperor of China, "there is no doctrine, and nothing holy about it." When a monk came to Hui Hai three hundred years later and asked to be instructed in the doctrine, Hui Hai replied "I have no doctrine to teach you."

Why is there no doctrine?

Because there is only the understanding that there is no entity to be "enlightened" or "liberated" by a doctrine.

That is the beginning, because without that understanding any method, practice, or teaching is at least a waste of time, and only reinforces the illusion of such an entity. And it is also the end because the profound understanding of that is the only "enlightenment" there could be.

What, then, could there be to teach, and who is there to be taught?

"I have no mouth, so how can I speak," said Hui Hai; "The Buddha taught for forty-nine years, yet no word was spoken," said Huang Po; "I travelled a thousand *li,* yet I have never taken a step," said another.

All such statements point to the same essential understanding, which is the beginning and the end.

91 ~ Finding the Seeker—A Dialogue

Looking for something?

Yes, spectacles.

You will never find them.

Why not?

Unless you are wearing them you cannot see them. And if you are wearing them you are looking through them.

Then I can find them though I cannot see them?

Alas, no.

How so?

You cannot find the found.

What is the found?

The seeking.

Why is that?

All seeking is just seeking—no matter what is sought.

You mean that whatever the object—it is always the same?

Always the same—and it isn't one.

Then what is it? The seeker?

There is no seeker.

But what is seeking?

The sought.

92 ~ *Whole-Mind*

Four Indications

I. DREAMING MIND
II. TAO, OR THE WAY IT IS
III. OBITUARY AND HEREAFTER
IV. WHAT WE MEAN BY "NOUMENON" AND "PHENOMENA"

I. Dreaming Mind

THE PAST, like the future, is in fact a dream-structure: sleeping or "waking," night or day, we dream both. Is that not obvious? Then when are we not dreaming?

In the present? Whenever could that be? Anything it could be is long passed before the processes of perception that conception can be completed. So that is entirely imagined, and therefore all three are conceptual.

We are whatever-we-are *here* and *now,* and forever. Time and space are our objectivisations. We make up all this nonsense—"dream" it as we say—and believe it to be fact—or what we call "real"!

"Whatever-we-are"? Yes, of course, but not what we have been misled to believe that we are. That was a composition, concepts actualised in mind; it was our living-dream, and the apperceiving of this is surely apperceiving what we were when dreaming and acting all the parts in our dream of "life" and "death" in a time-context.

We have never been anything else but the dreaming of our "lives"! What else could there be for us to be? That is also why what-we-are cannot be any objective *thing* soever.

This is our "nature" of which the Chinese masters speak so often, and which they strive so continually to enable us to envisage.

In Ch'an this would be called "Prajña," the functioning aspect of "Dhyana" as which we are potential only. This essential differentiation between immanence and transcendence, inseparable noumenally but conceptually apart, does not seem to be apparent in Vedanta.

II. Tao, or the Way It Is

I—as "me"—am whatever is perceived and conceived as "you": "you" and "it" are what is perceived and conceived soever.

There is no "I," no "you," no "it." We are the perceiving and conceiving which as perceptions conceived are then so-labelled as objects.

"We" as such, as any "thing," as any factual object, are not at all.

Therefore there can not be any such thing as *an* "I" perceiving and conceiving. Since there is not any entity to be cognised, there can not be any entity to cognise. This is why cognising can not be cognised, and this is why cognising—"Mind" in Buddhism, "Consciousness" in Vedanta, "Tao" in China, "the Holy Spirit" in Christianity, any of the names of "Allah" in Sufism, are just symbols whereby the phenomenal manifestation of "cognising" may be indicated in a spatio-temporal context.

If, in our spatio-temporal context, we were to "speak" among our mutually apparent "selves" on the noumenal level of this understanding, each of us would speak from the knowledge that each "other" had no existence but his appearance in the mind of each, which ultimately, as "I," is not plural, which is not singular either, but the conceiving of which in split-mind is necessarily multiple.

In practice this means that whatever conception A has of B, C has of B, B has of B (his "self") is all that B is or could be at that moment of "time." There can be no entity to be anything other than conceptual at any moment of time, for there is only cognising and neither cognising nor cognition can have an "ens."

A conceptual objectification in mind is that only and no sort of factual "thing," no example of which has ever existed other than as an appearance in a spatio-temporal context in what is called "mind" or "consciousness," which are symbols for the cognising process, itself a conceptual manifestation in imagined space-time.

Symbols themselves have no "ens," and it is idle to seek for anything conceptual that could express what is cognising, for cognising cannot cognise what is cognising, since no "thing" IS cognising.

Why is this so? It is so because cognising seems to occur in what is conceptualised as space-time, which is to say that it manifests in spatio-temporal extension, which implies that its objects can be visualised in "space" and have duration in "time," the whole of which conceptual processes are what we have to describe as subjective functioning—the subjective functioning of cognising itself.

Cognising, like the other five faculties of sentience, is in fact a dualistic expression of consciousness, of being conscious, which is the prajnatic aspect of *dhyana.* As conscious*ness* it is phenomenal, as *dhyana* it is noumenal. As the latter, phenomenally regarded, it is unconscious.

Therefore what-we-are noumenally does not appear (is not phenomenal), and so is referred to negatively as unconsciousness, no-mind (Buddhism), or deep-sleep (Vedanta).

Nothing further can be said, for all "saying" is expressed cognition, i.e. is dualised as subject/object conceptualising by means of the relativity of opposing and interdependent counterparts. Apart from that, all that ever was, ever is, ever will be, is pure undivided noumenality, apperceiving, entirely spontaneous, phenomenally transcendent and indescribable in dualistic terminology.

Certainly available, this apperceiving cannot be produced or acquired by any means whatever subject to space-time limitations, but the basic reason for this we can guess, which is that it is what we are, all that we are, and, being it, we cannot possibly know it subject to the limitations of the dualised process of objectification.

III. Obituary

The so-called "Truth" is beyond all the positive nonsense we talk and write. We never dive nearly deep enough into the abyss of negation, for such "truth" is beyond all forms of mental activity.

Negation is negative positivity.

Until negation is negated—thought is still present. The

absence of consciousness is still the presence of unconsciousness. Only in the absence of both positive and negative consciousness is the absence of the Absolute absolutely absent.

The "Truth" is the absolute absence of any kind of truth.

Presence and absence are dual aspects of appearance.
An absolute is positive and present.
There IS no presence, there IS no absence,
Both are positive phenomenal concepts.

Is and is-not are positive and negative isness,
But no form of isness IS.
All saying is thinking, all thinking is mental activity.
Only absolute absence is beyond phenomenality.

Hereafter

A long and arduous journey? Indeed, no! Rather is it total absence of displacement.

Why is that? Because there is neither place nor placed to displace!

Impossibly difficult? Indeed, no! All phenomenality, all positivity, all negation, are conceptually dependent on extension in space and duration.

And so? The space-time continuum is a bubble that bursts in the vacuum of total negation.

Without Here or There, Was or Will be,
When or Why, Who or What,
Suchness is Such.

Behind the beyond? There is no before to have a behind,
No thing to be beyond any or no thing.

Absolute negation of appearance, total phenomenal absence,
Is *"The Truth of Tao,"*
And there is nowhere else for it to be
But wherever I am.

IV. What We Mean by "Noumenon" and "Phenomena"

The phenomenal is whatever appears, whatever is present, whatever is not absent. Phenomenally, therefore, noumenality, which is not apparent as such, is absent.

Noumenally, however, phenomenality is not present, nor is it absent; it could be called potential. It is not as such, so it is neither present nor absent; the only being of phenomenality is noumenal.

And "noumenon," which is the Principal of potentiality which is appearance, can have no conceptual or objective existence, being a symbol for the origin of conceiving as such.

93 ~ The Meaning of Ch'an

THE FUNCTIONING of Prajña as non-volitional action is Dyhana and so is *being* Dyhana, since it *is Dyhana apparently functioning sequentially in time.*

When we look for Dyhana it is Prajña that is looking sequentially for what itself *is* non-sequentially. When we look for Prajña it is Prajña that is looking sequentially for itself as Dyhana. But neither can be seen, because in both cases Prajña is looking for what it is *which is what is looking as Prajña.*

That is why and how the sought is the seeker, and the seeker is the sought, and the seen is the see-er, and the see-er is the seen.

Intemporality or Dyhana is non-extension,

Temporality—prajñatic manifestation in seriality—is extension (in space-time).

"Seeing into the self" or into "self-nature" (which means the nature of *nature,* the "self" of *nature*) is not seeing any "thing": it is a pure act-of-seeing: see-ing=functioning= being. Functioning is Prajña, self-nature. The act of functioning, not what is apparently done, is Prajña or what-I-am, i.e. Dyhana, all functioning that is functional and not volitional.

This is the meaning of Ch'an.

All such functioning is Prajña-the-seeker *finding* Dyhana-the-sought, for functioning is the sequential *being* of Dyhana which is intemporality, so that functioning (Prajña) is seeking and finding that temporality and the intemporal are not separate.

But functioning here is apparently "being functioned"—or function functioning in "us"—for there is no one to "function," and thinking (like functioning) is "being thought"—or thought thinking in "us"—i.e. "pure" or spontaneous thought, or inseeing. That is the see-ing which is be-ing and act-ing—three apparent modes of sequentiality which are also intemporal.

Note: There can be no such thing (phenomenally) as "understanding the meaning of Ch'an," for understanding this is not-understanding it (dualistically).

Intemporality is "vertical" to temporality which is "horizontal," or, more precisely, dimensionally at right-angles to all three directions which constitute our concept of "volume" as which all phenomena appear.

Searching is finding—*finding that there is nothing to find.* The ultimate negation *can only be* the negation of duration, both positive and negative. There is nothing beyond to negate, for the negator is thereby negated, and therewith all answers to all questions.

Portrait of a Ch'anist (Tao-Buddhist)

If it's a concept—he bows and *smiles,*
If it isn't—there's nothing to smile at,
And no one to bow.

94 · The Supreme Vehicle Is . . .

THE SUPREME Vehicle is total negation of both elements of all possible contradictories (opposites), of *all* concepts and their counterparts.

It negates both positive and negative: it negates negation *itself.* Resolutely and finally, in one completed gesture, it turns away from all statements and conclusions soever. Objectification is seen as objecti-fiction—and is once and for all wiped out.

This is true-seeing, whole-seeing, and liberation from all that constituted bondage, for negation is seen to be the true nature of illusory phenomena, which is void, and by means of Negation is that seen.

No elements of binding remain, for all binding is conceptual. Nor is there freedom—since there is no nonconceptual entity to be free, nor anything binding from which to be unbound. So that total phenomenal negation (absence) is found to be total noumenal affirmation (presence).

Negation is the truth, by knowing which we can be aware of what-we-are in the act of knowing what we-are-not.

Note: The above is not only the heart of Buddhism, an epitome of the Madhyamika, and stated in the Heart Sutra, but the Maharshi—shortly before his death, and using three interdependent counterparts—said:

There is neither Creation nor Destruction,
Neither Destiny nor Free-will,
Neither Path nor Achievement;
This is the final Truth.

To confirm it would be presumptuous, to re-state it is a duty, to understand it is liberation.

95 · True-Seeing—A Dialogue

Hello! What are you worried about?

How do you know I am worried?

God, or whoever it was, gave you a face for some reason or other?

Birds not caught! My only "face" is the original one that I had before my father and mother were born—and it can't look worried!

Right! And the worry?

I've come to the conclusion, and finally, that Bob what's-his-name is not only a bore, but a mean and selfish sort of bastard!

Don't you agree?

Why should I? You describe *your* Bob what's-his-name: *mine* is not likely to be identical.

Damn it all, there is only one Bob in question, and we are both talking about him!

I am unable to agree! There are as many Bob what's-his-names as there are people who know him, plus one.

Metaphysically speaking perhaps, but the familiar phenomenal Bob is surely whatever he is!

Nonsense! There is no such being. What you are referring to is absolutely no thing whatever; "he" is as devoid of objective existence as anyone else.

As you or me?

Of course.

Then what is he?

He is an image in mind. You have just described what he is according to your image. In my image he appears slightly different, and less objectionable. His own "Bob"—as he appears to himself—is probably the hell of a fine fellow!

But there must be something that he really is!

Nothing whatever, absolutely *no thing*. He has, rigorously, no objective existence or being. He is only appearances in mind, interpreted diversely in a space-time context.

But whose appearances?

Ours: he appears to each of us as each of us sees him. What else is there for him to be?

Very well, but his? His own appearance to himself?

That also is a concept, nothing but a concept—his is not different in kind, but only in interpretation. You are supposing that his own is something factual, but it is not.

Would anyone believe that?

Probably not—unless he saw it. Conditioning is too strong.

Then who could take it?

It is not a dose of salts! Just an almost painfully obvious fact.

To whom?

Only to whoever can see that it must be so, that so it is, that it is fundamental, the very heart of how things are.

And when he sees it, what then?

If he really sees it—for hearing it or reading it is not seeing that so it is—he surely at the same time sees through everything that needs to be seen through—for all the rest follows.

Each of us needs to see it for himself and in his own way?

Each of us knows it for himself—if he is looking from the right direction.

And what is that?

From whole-mind, always from whole-mind.

Can one always do that?

Once should be enough. Let this one be it. It is better than all the ko-ans and co-nundrums that have ever been invented.

Why is that?

There is nothing artificial about it! It is just plain true-seeing.

96 ·- The Answer - II—A Dialogue

I. Clearing the Ground

IF WE can forget, or ignore, what we are not, we will find that we are what we have always been.

We cannot *find* what we are, because that is what we *are* and not what we are *not*.

Nor can we *know* what we are, because we are not somebody else who could know *us*.

What could there be to look for, what could there be to find? We are not double so that one of us could look for and find the other! The game of hide-and-seek needs two to play it.

Therefore whenever we look for what-we-are it can only be what-is-being-sought which is searching for what itself is. Have we ever seen a kitten succeed in catching her own tail?

Since however, absolutely, there cannot be any relative entity either to seek or to find, all that can be apperceived is *being aware* of what in space-time relativity is cognised as "seeking." But "seeking" is a concept extended in space-time, whose conceptual counterpart is "finding," the mutual negation of which, leaves nothing to seek or to be found, and being aware of the total absence of relativity is what is signified by the verbal symbol called Absolute.

II. The Answer

Can I be what I am?

Surely not! How could I?

Not you! I.

As I said.

How tiresome you can be! I was not referring to you but to myself.

There is no such entity—that is only an image in mind.

Very well, but I don't want to go into *that.*

You can't: you are already in it.

All right then; can I *be* it?

Since you are it, what is there to "be"?

So that "to be" is being it?

Precisely! Any kind of action would need someone to do it.

And "being" is an action?

If it were not a concept of doing something you would not have raised that pseudo-question.

"Being" is necessarily an action?

It is a concept, a movement in mind. Moreover it requires duration in conceptual space-time!

So I cannot "be" what I am?

What I am needs no "being."

I just ruddy-well *am?*

Need you think *it, let alone say it?*

Then I am nothing?

Not at all!

Then I must be something?

Neither any nor no "thing."

Just "am-ness"?

Certainly not!

Why so?

Any kind of "-ness" is necessarily a concept of some "thing," conceptually extended in space and in duration.

Cannot a concept suggest what it is not?

Negatively, yes; otherwise words would be useless metaphysically. But "-ness" implies some "thing" which is supposed to exist.

But I must—absolutely—*be!*

Not if you think *so.*

Why not?

Because if you "think so" there is an entity "so thinking," conceptually extended in "time" and in "space."

Impossible chap to talk to! Impossible to get an answer!

Absolutely, of course: there would need to be *"an answer" and "someone" to give it.*

And there are such only in relativity?

At last! there cannot be a relative answer to a question that is not relative.

But you admitted just now that a negative concept can suggest what it is not.

That is because a concept, being relative, is relative to what it is absolutely.

Then any concept can be true!

Absolutely, not relatively.

If that is so, wherein is its truth to be found?

Relatively in mutual negation of its relative factors, absolutely in finding that you are aware of that negating as such.

Such finding-that-you-are-aware being so-to-speak "basic"?

Absolutely ultimate and ultimately absolute.

And concepts can lead to that?

Negatively, yes—if the negation also be negated.

Why should that be?

Because, then, no trace of relativity can remain.

Leaving absolute absolutely present?

Neither present nor absent—for they too are relative.

As for instance? . . .

"I neither am nor am not."

Which means? . . .

Neither either nor neither.

Which cannot be conceived?

Can it?

Surely not. So that reveals it?

I do not think so.

Then what does?

The resulting frustration perhaps?

Which is failure?

Failure, or success, of what?

That which was trying to conceive.

There was no entity to do that.

Then what was there?

Was there not a "trying," in suppositional space-time?

Yes.

What was "trying"?

Whatever failed.

There was a "failing," in space-time?

Of course.

What was aware *of "failure" in space-time?*

I was.

. . .

Why don't you answer?

"You" cannot.

Why not?

Because "you," whatever it may be, being an object, is always conceptually extended in space-time.

And so?

Only I am—whoever may represent what I am objectively, that is to say—subject to spatio-temporal extension.

Which latter is relativity?

Which is what relativity is.

But relativity is whatever is relative to Absolute.

Whatever is relative to absolute is so by such conceptual extension contrasted with that of its opposite.

Mutually interdependent in their conceptual extension?

Quite so.

And their mutual negation abolishes their mutual extension?

Inevitably.

So that it is abolition of conceptual extension in space-time which abolishes relativity?

Undoubtedly.

Revealing what-we-are, timeless and infinite, void in nonextension, and so absolute?

No comment is required.

Then why don't you teach this?

I don't teach anything. What is there to teach?

Why is it not taught by others?

Direct-seeing cannot be taught, and relative teaching is bound by tradition.

Traditional teaching is diffuse and confusing, complicated and overlaid with defunct verbiage and outlived concepts.

I bow.

Whereas this is simple, clear, and obvious.

I prostrate.

So what?

Apprehend extension—that should suffice.

Unextended—we can "be"?

Unextended in conceptual space-time we cannot not "be"—we ARE.

97 ⋅ Awareness

I

IF I AM awake—who could there be to know it? The dreamer is asleep.

There is no I to be asleep or awake. An "I" is a stooge. Whenever I say "I," implying an entity, a stooge is speaking,

II

Relatively "awareness" is being aware of some "thing." Calling that thing a "self" or "myself" makes it no whit less an object of a subject. Awareness of no thing is also awareness of a "thing"—that kind of thing which is "no thing." "Pure" awareness, non-objective awareness, is non-awareness: if it implies self-awareness it is awareness of an objective "self."

If I am aware of what I am, then what I am is the object of a subject that is aware of an object, and it is then an object of which a subject is aware—and so on *ad infinitum* in a perpetual regression. What I am, therefore, cannot be aware.

This applies equally to an alternative term such as "consciousness." It is impossible to be aware of what is being aware, or to be conscious of what is being conscious.

It follows, as far as dialectic thought is concerned, that there cannot be any objective "thing" that is conscious or aware, which requires that being conscious or being aware as such cannot have any objective existence. Phenomenally being conscious, aware, is only a concept. It can be referred to symbolically, for instance as "noumenon," but it does not phenomenally exist.

That is why dualistically I am not, why I cannot possibly be.

That also is why the only possible evidence for such a supposition as "I" is the phenomenon of all appearance. That is why a Schrödinger can state that Consciousness is a singular of which the plural is unknown. A metaphysical Master, however, such as Shen Hui, must insist that consciousness is not a "singular" either. In other words, as a concept it can dialectically be assumed because it is the only possible dialectical explanation of any appearance at all or of any manifestation whatever.

This is of no importance? It is of the greatest possible importance. It proves that as conscious and rational entities, entities rationally knowing what rationally can be known, we cannot possibly exist.

III

Metaphysically this implies that we cannot not-exist either. And for the same reason. Absence of positive existence comports also absence of its counterpart, negative existence—that kind of existence which is non-existence, i.e. total absence of both negative and positive concepts.

What we are, then, is total absence of the presence of both positive and negative awareness, which is total absence of the presence of both positive and negative existence, which is total absence of both positive and negative presence, which is absence of absence as well as of presence.

Dialectically this establishes the fact that we cannot be anything that we could ever imagine ourselves to be—in the singular or in the plural—for what we are cannot be anything that could be objectively visualised by the split mind of dialectic reasoning.

What, then, is this great and obscure mystery that we neither are nor are not conceptually? No mystery at all! It is what divided mind cannot know because it is divided into subject and object. So divided it can reason, but it cannot apperceive its indivision, its own wholeness, which is all that it is and all that we can be.

Note: The notion of "non-objective awareness" may appear to equate with the "third state" of Vedanta, popularly referred to as "deep sleep," during which phenomenal or apparent existence disappears. But what-we-are is beyond that, as Sri Ramana Maharshi stated in his *Supplement to the Forty Verses,* No. 32, referred to as the "transcendent state" beyond Deep Sleep, Dreaming Sleep, and Waking Sleep.

98 ∽ "Seeing—Seeing—Seeing"

Jalalu'ddin Rumi

I

All see-ing occurs in mind.
Where do "you" occur?
Where do "I" occur?
Where does "he," "she," "it" occur?
Only in mind that is looking.

Who sees?
Do not I see, always I?
But I cannot see my seeing,
Hear my hearing, taste my tasting,
Smell my smelling, feel my touching.
Nor can I cognise my cognising of any of these.

Therefore I am absent, always absent.
I only appear to exist as an object in mind.
I am not "here" or "there" except as a concept.

Who sees "me," who sees "us," via one another
We who are absent as see-ers?
I, absent, see us all via each object seen as "us,"
And what is seen is not, can never be, us,
But always, and only, what is looking,

Mind which is looking,
Looking via conditioned objects
Perceiving each "other" in mind,
Not one of which has any existence as "other."

❧

That is why there are no "others,"
Because, being absent,
No "I" is present.

II

Comment

When you look at me it is in "your" mind that I appear to exist.

When "I" look at you it is in "my" mind that you appear to exist.

When each of us looks at the other it is in the mind of the "looker" that whatever is seen appears.

Everything we may think of one another only appears to exist in the mind in which it appears.

And nothing we attribute to one another exists objectively at all.

"Your" mind is only apparently "yours."

It is not "yours" but what you are, all that you are.

Its "looking" is all "looking," see-ing-as-such manifesting relatively as subject perceiving object.

Note: Asked to state briefly what I believe to be the basic factor of what "all the sages of all the ages" were seeking to impart within the idiomatic and other limitations of their time and circumstances, this is approximately what I should reply, expressed in our own idiom.

ꕥ

Wheresoever, whensoever, whosoever says "I"
I say it.

99 - *Absolutely*

I

THERE HAS never been anything objective whatsoever.

There has never been anything sensorially perceptible; there is not and there never will be.

There has never been a "space" within which any perceptible object could be extended so that it could be perceived.

There has never been a "time" during which any perceptible object could have the sequential duration necessary for its perceiving.

For there has never been an *entity*—without which no object whatever could be created, perceived, or cognised as an object.

II

No object has any existence other than that of a percept conceptualised in mind.

Mind also has no existence other than that of a conceptualised percept.

This statement has no existence other than that of a conceptualised percept.

Who made the statement?

What do you mean by "Who?"? "Who?" also is only a conceptualised percept, and there never was one outside mind, nor any "Who?" to ask the question, nor any "Who?" to answer it.

"Who?" is a figure of speech, a theoretical image, a symbolical personification.

III

What, then, is there?

How could there be any such question to answer when there cannot be any subject to ask, any question to be asked, or any object to answer?

The presence of the concept of an answer would constitute bondage to relativity.

The absence of such a concept would maintain bondage to relativity.

But the absence of both question and answer, connoting the absence of any *entity* to ask or not to ask, to answer or not to answer, must constitute release from relativity.

For no entity is there either to be bound or free.

IV

There has never been anything objective—and yet there is no subject either? It is because there has never been anything objective that there cannot be a subject. "A subject" would necessarily be an object of another subject, and so on in a perpetual regression.

So there has never been a subject, and therefore there has never been an object—except conceptually in mind, whereby every apparent object has a subject which thereby is the object of another subject; and *the perpetual regression of this process* is conceptualised by each of us as "I."

V

There has never been an object because there has never been a subject, and there has never been a subject because there has never been an object. Phenomena are conceptual because they result from this illusory process which is a perpetual regression.

Therefore this perpetual regression is the mechanism of phenomenality, and regression and phenomenality are inseparable and cannot be differentiated.

This inexistence of phenomenality, consequent upon the absence of a subjective factor which could be such without thereby becoming an object, constitutes relativity. By this relativity we reason, and nothing we can know can be known otherwise, for the result of this relative reasoning is what we know as "knowledge."

VI

In knowing that "knowledge" must be relative we must also know, for we cannot avoid this knowledge, that in order that our knowledge may be relative there must also be knowledge that is absolute, without which relativity could not be relative.

But absolute knowledge we cannot know; we can neither know it nor in any way possess it. What is the reason of this inability? The answer to this question is obvious—though it cannot be established by means of relative reasoning.

The answer is that we can neither know nor possess what we know must inevitably be absolute because this absolute, which cannot be denied or in any way negated, must be, and is, a symbol for what we ourselves are.

VII

Phenomenally absolutely absent, noumenally we are absolutely present. Our absolute unicity remains despite its phenomenal division into relative duality.

In space-time absolutely transcendent, we are immanent in sentience, and all manifestation manifests our absolute absence.

Integrated or disintegrated our presence is absolute as I.

Note: Dialectically it would be maintained that because the relative requires an absolute therefore an absolute requires the relative in order to be absolute at all. "An absolute" thereby becomes a conceptual object and requires a subject like any other member of a pair of interdependent counterparts in the mechanism of relative reasoning.

This, of course, is correct, but it is also begging the question, since dialectically dialectics could never transcend dialectics. But metaphysically it is not a fact at all. What it does is to lead dialectic reasoning—the reasoning of mind divided into subject and object—to its self-imposed limits, the limits imposed by its own premises. The ultimate pair of counterparts are "the conceivable" and "the inconceivable," and it points beyond, to the negation of both counterparts, which negation defines an order of mind no longer divided but whole. (This applies also to the pair of counterparts represented by the concepts of phenomenality and noumenality; this syllogism also is conceptual, but it points beyond all conceptuality, both positive and negative conceptuality, and such transcendence is represented by the symbol termed "Noumenon.")

To imagine that it could be possible to reach that which cannot be conceived by means of conceptual reasoning is surely otiose. What can be done, and what Nagarjuna and his school did so magisterially, is to prove conceptually the ultimate falsehood of all concepts, be they never so holy. He went no further, but not because he could see no further—as appears to be the case with some of his commentators. He went to the limits imposed by his self-imposed premises—those of then, and still, contemporary dialectics, but his ultimate virtue was that he saw clearly what lay beyond, that is to what his dialectics pointed, and their sole justification. To some others "that" has always been seen as absolute nothingness for, as "that," nothing it was, but to him and to those who understood him it was also the source and origin of absolutely everything which was, is, and ever could *appear to be* any "thing" at all.

"The Absolute"

It is often said that "the Absolute" is hidden, but nothing could be more untrue.

What we are as "I" is everywhere and always. "I" cannot hide: from whom could "I" be hidden? To play hide-and-seek with myself is a game that even small children do not play.

100 ⁓ Quips and Queries - VI

DISCURSIVE THOUGHT is transcended, and the Absolute is reached, through negation.

Sunya (Void, Emptiness) only means that nothing can be said about this to which it refers.

Noumenality knows no I.

Not only can we not communicate directly and only via our common central non-being, but all that we are is that common central non-being.

All phenomena are mind.
Mind is all phenomena.
What else could either be?

The subjective is whatever you can't see because it is what is looking.

Fasting of the Mind
The cessation of thought is the continuation of silence.

Objectifying what is functioning (while objectifying) is all that "bondage" could be.

Colophon

I Do Not Believe . . .

I do not believe in the existence of any object, in the factual being of anything objective whatsoever.

I do not believe in the existence of anything that can be heard, seen, felt, smelled, tasted or cognised, which is sensorially perceived and conceptually interpreted as an object, nor in that of any dream, vision, hallucination, or other kind of living experience, whether empirically suffered in an apparently sleeping, waking, or drugged condition.

I do not believe in the existence, material or psychic, of any objective entity which might be supposed to be writing these lines, nor in the factual existence of the words with which they may appear to be written.

Why is this so? Firstly, and also finally:

I do not believe that whatever may appear to be subjected to extension in space and to succession in duration could be other than *an appearance in mind.*

Then who is responsible for this statement?

Who? I am responsible, as I am responsible for every appearance soever. And every other sentient phenomenon can say that also, or know it without being able to say it, every man and monkey, bird and beetle, reptile and rose.

For, in the voidness of basic nature, so it is—and I, whoever says it, am the immanence phenomenally whose transcendence noumenally is what I am.

Posthumous Postscript

Birthless and undying,
How could I "live"?
Never having "lived,"
How could I "die"?

Timeless and infinite,
Unextended in space-time,
Unliving, undying, Unbeing, I AM.

PPS. And so are you.

Note: "Birth-life-death" are concepts extended in a space-time context and experienced in mind like all psychic manifestations.

Appendix

QUOTATIONS

TECHNICAL TERMS

DEFINITIONS

SUGGESTIONS AND COMMENTS

COME TO THINK OF IT

What is NOT the Absolute?
What else could anything BE?

Quotations

Concerning "Enlightenment"

"If you practise MEANS of attaining Enlightenment for three myriad aeons but without losing your belief in something really attainable, you will still be as many aeons from your goal as there are grains in the sands of the Ganges.

"But if by direct apperception of the *Dharmakaya's* true nature you apperceive it in a flash, you will have reached the highest goal taught in the Three Vehicles. Why? Because the belief that the *Dharmakaya* can be attained belongs to the doctrines of those sects which do not understand the truth."

HUANG PO, *Wan Lin Record,* 49, p. 125

"A direct apperception of the Dharmakaya's true nature" implies immediate apperception of unicity with what is referred to as "The Dharmakaya"—which is our "true nature" and all that noumenally we are.

Note: "Something attainable" is necessarily *your* object, so that "attaining Enlightenment" implies "regarding Enlightenment as an object in mind." "The Dharmakaya's true nature" is what you are as I, so that a "direct apperception of that" is all that could be required. As an object it could never be "attained"—since it can have no objective quality whatever; as what is sought it is the seeker, and as the "seeker" it can never be found.

"Enlightenment" could only be a phenomenal experience of what-we-are.

The Ultimate

The ultimate is that "Enlightenment" means *neither* "enlightenment" *nor* "non-enlightenment"—which is *absence of an entity to conceive either.*

HUI HAI says that *Samyak-sambodhi* is the *identity* of form and void (voidness of form), whereas "Marvellous Enlightenment" is realisation of the absence of opposites, i.e. *neither* the one *nor* the other, as stated above. He also says that "in substance they are one." But their "sub-stance" is their mutual annihilation as opposing concepts.

Quotations

As the late ATMANANDA implied:

If what phenomenally we are is sentience,
Then Awareness-of-Sentience must surely be our noumenal being.
But such awareness must not be conceptualised as such.

He also stated that "Consciousness, mistakenly conditioned by time, appears as thought."

If so, that may be why thought is notoriously the obstacle?

He maintained that when it is seen that the content of thought is nothing but consciousness, thought vanishes and consciousness alone remains.

He also implied that if sound is the hearing of it, awareness of such hearing is what-I-am.

Objects, like the Absolute, can only be the cognising of them, and awareness of such cognising must be what-we-are.

"Transcendent to thought, the Absolute, however, is thoroughly immanent in experience. A critique of experience, like the Madhyamika dialectic, is conscious of this immanence, the phenomenalisation of the Absolute."

MURTI, *The Central Philosophy of Buddhism*, p. 141

We are experience (of sentience), for experience is sentience. We do not experience: we *are* experience. Phenomenally all we are is empirical sentience in a time-context, sequential experienc*ing*.

❧

There is no (phenomenal) activity called "seeing." Therefore see-*ing* is noumenal. Nagarjuna maintains that this must be so, since an eye cannot see itself and, unable to see itself, could not see other than self. (*Madhyamika Karikas* III, 4-5). This has already been pointed out, but the famous philosopher's way of establishing it is important.

Non-Duality

As the *Bhagavad Gita* says, by whatever means and in whatever the dividual approaches the in-dividual—in that way the undivided will come to him.

The direct and immediate *means* is the Negative *way*, which reveals instantly that there has never been *division*.

But neither in fact "approaches" the other, for the apparent advance of the phenomenal is the apparent approach of the noumenal, like a man walking towards his own reflection in a mirror. Intemporal Presence is found to be present at one moment of spatio-temporal functioning.

The term "individual" is here correctly used, i.e. to meant

what it says. Therefore it does not describe a phenomenon divided into subject-and-object as in colloquial usage, which should be called a "dividual." The term "individual" indicates the Absolute.

ꙮ

"Perceptions employed as a base for building up positive concepts are the origin of all ignorance."

"Apperceiving that there is nothing to perceive is deliverance." (Hui Hai, p. 48)

ꙮ

Having ideas about "a way" is making an object of what you are, which could not be an objective "way."

"I am the Way"—whoever says it—as Jesus stated. This is the Sublime Way, also called Tao.

Let Us Listen to Huang Po

"If only you have a tacit understanding of Mind,
You will not need to search for any Dharma,
For then Mind is the Dharma."

Chun Chou Record, p. 48

"There is just a mysterious tacit understanding,
And no more."

p. 45

"It is void, omnipresent, silent, pure;
It is glorious and mysterious peaceful joy,
And that is all."

p. 55

"The Wordless Dharma of the One Mind . . .
Those who should be tacitly Enlightened
Would arrive at the state of Buddhahood."

p. 52

"The Buddha, who broke down the notion of objective existence. . . ."

p. 56

Always "understanding," and always "tacit": "tacit" here means "unspoken."

❧

"There are no sentient beings to be delivered."

p.70

As stated also, in the same words, in the Diamond Sutra.

❧

"A transmission in concrete terms cannot be the Dharma. Mind is transmitted with Mind, and these Minds do not differ. . . . In fact, however, Mind is not Mind, and transmission is not transmission."

p. 50

The "true Dharma" is that there is no one to have a "Dharma"—true or untrue—nor any Dharma to have.

❧

"If even self has no objective existence, how much less has

other-than-self! Thus neither Buddha nor sentient beings exist objectively."

p. 70

What more do you want? There is no such thing as objective existence (other than conceptually, like any kind of dream or vision) and "Identification" is belief in conceptual existence as factual.

❧

"There are no 'Enlightened' men or 'ignorant' men, and there is no oblivion. 'Existence' and 'non-existence' are both empirical concepts no better than illusions."

p. 70

"'Buddha' and 'sentient Beings' are both your own false conceptions. It is because you do not know real Mind that you delude yourselves with such objective concepts."

p. 71

"The Buddha" is a concept. Mind must not be conceiv*ed:* conceiv*ing* is what it IS, Why? That which is conceived is conceived by a "you" or a "me": conceiv*ing* is the "mind" which is what we are.

❧

"Mind is not of several kinds, and there is no doctrine that can be put into words. As there is no more to be said, the Assembly is dismissed!"

p. 61

Self is not of several kinds either, nor different, and the Assembly is also therein. There cannot be anything that is not: the entire universe is in Mind, and nothing can appear otherwise than as a concept—some "thing" conceived by a "conceiver."

That, no doubt, is why "there is no doctrine that can be put into words."

"All *methods* of following the Way are ephemeral."

"There is absolutely nothing which can be obtained."

Wang Ling Record, p. 125

"No amount of seeking can ever lead to Mind."

p. 128

"You" cannot "see" (or "seek") it because "you" think "you" are looking, and "you" cannot *see* LOOKING, for *it* is what is looking, and what is looking is not "a" you. No "you" could ever see *it*. "You" removed—*it* is HERE.

"Finally remember that from first to last not even the smallest grain of anything perceptible has ever existed or ever will exist."

p. 127

"Every grain of matter, every appearance, is one with Eternality and Immutability."

p. 128

Superficially contradictory? Not at all! The first states that nothing phenomenal (no form of appearance) factually exists as an object; the second states that everything phenomenal (each appearance) is entirely noumenal, i.e. that it has no existence apart from its source which is all that it could be. And that "source" has no objective quality whatever, not even "existence."

"The way of the Buddhas flourishes in a mind utterly freed from conceptual thought-processes."

p. 127

Huang Po keeps on saying that "we" will never "reach Mind by means of Mind"—for what is *reaching* IS Mind anyhow.

We are trying to use Mind, but there is no "us" to do it, and Mind is what we are—a bit of a muddle, as you will admit. But if we can relinquish the idea of ourselves as a "self," and thereby re-become "Mind"—we are likely to find that we are *what we are,* and thereby what we always were.

Technical Terms

The Use of the Term "Reality"

THE USE of the term "Reality" (thing-ness), inevitably implying some objective "thing," could never serve as an admissible indication of the totally unconditioned, which connotes absolute absence of objective quality. The phenomenal alone can be termed "real," and the noumenal "unreal."

Noumenally, however, to suppose that there could be any difference between what appears to be "real" and what appears to be "unreal," between some "thing" and no "thing," is ingenuous—since neither the one nor the other, both together or absence of both, could possibly have other than a conceptual existence.

Merit

Only unmerited consideration should be worth having. Why? Otherwise it is just getting your deserts. Then the giver is only doing his duty, fulfilling an obligation, protecting himself from blame for not performing a duty. For that no gratitude is due.

Unmerited, the giver gives freely, so that it is an honour to receive, and the receiver without merit owes gratitude to the giver. Then the obligation lies with him. Is it not nobler to be obliged than to be paid for services rendered?

Sages are unconscious of merit; pseudo-sages may claim it

and take it as due. The former do not enjoy it, and cannot feel that it is due. But they may know gratitude. Merit only exists as a concept.

Metaphysically speaking, the concept of merit can have no significance that is other than relative—since a factual entity would need to be posited in order to possess that attribute. It follows that the application of the term "merit" could only imply absence of an entity to have it, which should connote absolute humility in relativity.

Tao and Te

"TAO," as the first line of the *Tao Te Ching* declares, is not a name and may not be so understood. It is a verbal or auditive symbol indicating what as sentient beings we are, not relatively but absolutely. Any translation must necessarily be absurd.

As its use in the text amply reveals, the translation of "TE" as "Virtue" gives an entirely false impression of its sense, since that word has for us a moral implication, which could not be in question, and displaces the context from metaphysics into ethics. "Virtus" in the latin-derived languages means "value," "quality," "excellence," and here the only quality attributable to TAO is the "functioning" aspect thereof in relativity, whereby phenomena appear, which is called *Te.*

The meaning, therefore, of TAO TE CHING can only be "Scripture concerning TAO and (its) Functioning," which we can also describe as "Absolute and Relative," "Noumenon and the Phenomenal," "Dhyana and Prajna," "Brahman and Brahma," etc., etc.

The doctrine implied is universal, but its Taoist expression is earlier, clearer, and more concisely revealed. It represents the essential apprehension as well as the essential comprehension—which, ultimately, must be identical.

Note: Only a few specialists in China could be qualified to express an opinion concerning the precise meaning in modern languages of characters in Chinese script (which were "characters" and not "words" in our grammatical sense) as written in the sixth century B.C. Moreover in order to do so they would be relying on the use of such characters in Confucian and other ethical treatises and not on works dealing with Taoist metaphysics, of which there are none older than Chuang Tse and none as ancient as the *Tao Te Ching*. Therefore, where translation is concerned, precision must depend on apprehension of the text as a whole by whoever may be in a position to apprehend it.

信 心 銘

Note Concerning the Hsin Hsin Ming

This celebrated scripture is attributed to the Third Patriarch of Ch'an, SENG T'SAN, but was probably composed by an unspecified Master of the T'ang Dynasty.

The title, as usually translated—"Writing (concerning) Faith (or Belief) In Mind, or On The Believing Mind"—is quite inapposite and, if it were correct, would have to be attributed to a later editor, since untitled compositions were usual rather than exceptional in the earlier period in China. As this is one of the most perfect expositions of Ch'an at the height of its development, the title were better left untranslated—unless it be rendered as herein suggested.

If the last verse is understood, the meaning of the title *Hsin Hsin Ming* is revealed.

"Hsin hsin" is a cliche which is commonly rendered as

"faith" or "belief," but here it quite evidently implies "apperceiving," which gives, as title, "Scripture (concerning) Apperceiving" (or "Apperceiving-mind," although the redundancy is unjustifiable).

The last verse, so translated, then states—following Suzuki's text—

> "Apperceiving mind is not divided,
> Undivided, mind IS Apperceiving.
> This is where words fail,
> For it is not of the past, future, or present."

Or, following L. Wang and J.M.'s text in *Hermès* I—

> "L'esprit est indivis,
> Ce qui est divis n'est pas l'esprit-qui-s'aperçoit,
> Ici les voies du langage s'arrêtent
> Car il n'est ni passé, ni présent, ni futur."

The final verse, then, fully justifies the title, and the title recapitulates the last verse.

Note: The two words romanised as "hsin" represent, of course, totally different characters, one of which usually means "mind" or "heart" 心, specifically "Buddha-mind," the conjunction forming the cliché referred-to above. The available translations of the text, though of unusual quality and insight, are by no means definitive.

N.B. For readers unfamiliar with technical terms, "'apperception' is mind's perception of itself." *(The Concise Oxford Dictionary)*

Definitions

Methods and Practices

ECHOES? ALL echoes! Searching for the source of a sound by chasing its echo.

Not-Thinking

"I" cannot be thought: the thinking is what I am.
It is I who am the thinking of whatever is being thought.
And the not-thinking of whatever is not being thought.
It is I who am the doing of whatever is being done.
And the not-doing of whatever is not being done.
Being aware of this is called "Not-Thinking."

Definition Defined

Every objective description obscures whatever it endeavours to reveal which is beyond itself. That is to say that all verbal formulation of intuitional apprehension obscures rather than reveals what has been apperceived.

Freedom

As "that" there is no entity to be free; as "This" there is no entity to be bound.

What could be more simple and obvious?

"That"

The reason why "that" is the most mischievous word, metaphysically, in our language, is that it points towards what-we-are as an object of what-we-are-not, whereas the reverse is the precise truth. It is *néfaste* in that its use necessarily obliges the speaker to be speaking as a phenomenal object envisaging its own noumenality objectively, whereas the relative truth he is seeking is that *phenomena* are just the objectification of noumenon, and therefore are "that" whose *subject* is "this."

Dyana-Ch'an-Zen: Non-Conceptualised

The moment I cease to be my self,
I become what I am,
For I am that-I-am the moment I am no longer.
There is no "I," but I,
And that-I-am is I.

Pretty little phrases? Perhaps, but they can mean a lot, suggest more, and point to the centre of Infinity and Intemporality, but don't let us imagine that they say what cannot be said.

Ancient Advice to Devotees of the Golden Calf

P'an Yün, a lay scholar of course—nearly always the best—of the eighth century, friend and pupil of Ma Tsu, rather like Vimalakirti *vis-à-vis* the Buddha, left us a celebrated statement.

"Empty yourselves of everything that exists, and never reify *(shih)*—make a 'thing' of—anything that does not exist (phenomenally)."

"Void"

"The Void" is what you can't see
When you are looking for a self that isn't there.
Why is that?
Because it is what is looking.

Wu Wei

Our every self-conscious act is a *reaction* to a stimulus (via the sensory mechanism).

Therefore *wu wei* means "not-*re*acting,"
And *wei wu wei* means "acting (that is) not-*re*acting,"
Which is spontaneous acting,
Which is non-volitional acting,
Which is the essence of Taoism.

Bondage? Objectifying what I am as a subjective entity is making a "self" of what I am.

As soon as this concept becomes a reflex-action I am in bondage to that concept.

Liberation requires the abolition of that reflex-action, and the absence of positive or negative objectification of what-I-am. When what-I-am ceases to be a concept no bondage can remain—for then there is no longer a conceptual entity to be bound or to be free.

Such is the meaning of "I AM THAT I AM."

Bondage to a *guru,* even if described as "spiritual bondage," is maintained by chains as heavy as those suffered in any other category of servitude.

❧

Equanimity is incompatible with an I-concept.
An I-concept re-acts as "volition,"
Equanimity acts but does not re-act.
Equanimity—"mind that is equal"—is *neither* positive *nor* negative.
Reacting is re-action between positivity and negativity, between Yes and No.
If you reveal equanimity "you" cannot "have" it; you must be it.
Then Yes and No have no meaning.

"Mind" Our Own Business

Phenomena ARE "mind,"
All that is sensorially-perceived IS "mind,"
And we are the perceiving sentience

Sentience as such is phenomenal experience of "mind,"
And "mind" means, and is, noumenon

The apparent existence of phenomena
Is the apparent existence of "mind,"
But we can only be conscious of "mind,"
When we become aware of noumenal presence,
Using the word "I" to indicate our phenomenal absence.

Preposterous? The two best examples of *pre-post*ering?
The American definition of Ch'an as "Chinese Zen"? or a definition of Judaism as "Jewish Christianity"? Twins, or just sibs?

The Positive Way? 1. There is one, yes indeed—but apt to be ineffective until one's boot-laces snap with the weight of one's own uplift.

Missing It

What you are trying to see is what is looking! What else could there be for you to see? What else could you never see?
We all miss it because "we" are there to miss it.
If "we" were not present who would there be to miss it, since it is what "we" are?

"THAT" points outwards to some "thing" *there,*
"THIS" points inwards to some "thing" *here.*
But one-and-all I am, and neither,
Being no *thing* at all.

The Soft Answer

It takes two to quarrel—and there is nobody here.

Volition? Volition is as conditioned as any other factor in

the performance of an action.

The Answer to Every Question

"Conceptual absence of 'neither Yes nor No'" should be the most concise and least inaccurate statement of *the double negative of Shen Hui.*

Suggestions and Comments

The Blessed

WHAT ALL our decadent religions need—and they all *are* decadent to-day—is not a Congregation of Saints, but a Congregation of Debunkers.

After which Augean operation they should once again reveal, rather than obscure, so that in the *absence* of the ordinal we may find the *presence* of the cardinal.

Idolatry

Affective fixation on the personality of a master, teacher, *guru,* is a serious obstacle to "liberation": the person of the liberator becomes the gaoler.

The Chinese Buddhist Masters told their monks to kill the Buddha if by chance they met him. That was the reason. But were they themselves able to avoid taking the place of the Buddha?

The personality of the master, apparently inherent or projected on to him, is the most serious, constant, and insuperable hindrance to the success of his own work, and perhaps the most urgent and difficult of his technical problems. None such who ignores it can, in fact, be a Master.

He is at most a vehicle, yet he is interpreted and regarded as the source of what he is teaching. He may say that he has nothing to teach, but he is not believed; that he has nothing to give, but his words are scorned; that he himself has no existence as such, still less as a Master, and he is praised for "humility" and his words are discounted.

How can he succeed in face of this blind craving for idolatry, for worshipping an objective idol, which conceptual image directly inhibits everything which he is endeavouring to impart, and which contradicts and undermines the life-work to which he is consecrated?

Note: Such an idolator has not understood enough even to ask himself "*Who* is trying to worship *what?*"

Come to Think of It

My absence here is my presence everywhere
For total absence is ubiquituous presence.

"No 'experience' is of any value which is not experience of what you are as I."

No doubt—but can there be any other kind of experience?

Who are you? You don't shave your *self,* do you?
You shave what you see in the mirror!
Noticing that is the "Negative Way."

Time? What time is—I am.

Father Time? Yes, time is indeed our father, as of all appearances in space, and space is our mother. Why?

Without them none of us would be perceptible or "here." But as a Supreme Authority once remarked, "I and My Father are One."

The Positive Way? 2. It is going on wearing your mask and domino after the ball is over. Whereas *the Negative Way* is removing your disguise and revealing your true identity while the ball is still in progress.

"Death" is nonsense: what is there to die?
"Life"? How could "life" "die"? That is a contradiction
in terms. Can "light" become "darkness"?
"Light" can only cease to be apparent.

Is liberation possible?
There would have to be freedom
In order that bondage might be,
And an entity to know either.
That is the answer.

Activity-without-attachment is non-volitional living.

However could "being" be plural, or I-ness singular?

Every thing empirically "known" is—appearance.

If "thinking" is what you *are*—can "you" be "*the* thinker"?

❧

There has never been a phenomenal subject:
The notion is nonsense.

❧

Communion with your Godhead (not what is *commonly* called "prayer") should give you the understanding or inseeing which you seek, according to your capacity to receive it.

❧

Reflection

What we see in the mirror does not shave This which is shaving it.

Yet our daily life is based on that very *illusion!*

Note: We think this is shaving itself? Yes—but when we consider the matter we find that there isn't one.

❧

What I am is both transcendent and immanent.

❧

You are what I am,
I am what you are,
I am what God is,
God is what we are?
Yes: if we sing it.

The Positive Way - 3

"Nearer my tail to thee," the kitten remarked—as with a final desperate leap she overreached herself and fell head-over-heels into the pond.

ꕥ

"The Void" can only imply "this which is unobjectivisable"—and "this" because it is what is objectivising.

ꕥ

I who am light, how could I know darkness?
For wherever I am darkness cannot be.

ꕥ

Noumenon, after all, is what phenomenality IS
And all that relativity IS—is Absolute.

大 疑

Only by "failure" can I succeed

Note: Rinzai "Zen"? Yes, on account of the artificial use, or misuse, made of it in *ko-ans.* But the inherent truth is universal. The verb "succeed" is used in its primary and transitive sense implying "succession." In Ch'an it is represented by *Ta I*—translated as "Great Doubt," describing the phenomenal reaction of divided mind to the threat of reintegration.

This ends our work? So it does! Are you, perhaps, wondering why? There might be a reason?

Index

Words representing the subject of chapters will be found in the Table of Contents.

Words which form the essential subject of this book and occur in the majority of chapters are only indexed in exceptional cases.

References are to numbered chapters: "n" indicates "Note"; where they are in the Appendix or front matter they are marked "p" (page); subsections of chapters are indicated by Roman numerals.

The aim of this index is to enable readers to find a chapter in which they remember some technical term, name, or other mnemonic feature.

Index

Index

Other Spiritual Classics by Wei Wu Wei

Fingers Pointing Towards the Moon, Foreword by Ramesh S. Balsekar

The first book by Wei Wu Wei, who wrote it because "it would have helped the pilgrim who compiled it if it had been given to him."

ISBN 1-59181-010-8 • $16.95

Why Lazarus Laughed

Wei Wu Wei explicates the essential doctrine shared by the traditions of Zen Buddhism, Advaita, and Tantra, using his iconoclastic humor to drive home his points.

ISBN 1-59181-011-6 • $17.95

Ask the Awakened, Foreword by Galen Sharp

This book asserts that there are no Buddhist masters in present western society, and we must rely on the teachings of the ancient masters to understand Buddhism.

ISBN 0-9710786-4-5 • $14.95

The Tenth Man, Foreword by Dr. Gregory Tucker

In giving us his version of the perennial philosophy, Wei Wu Wei brings a very different perspective to the conventional notions about time, love, thought, language, and reincarnation.

ISBN 1-59181-007-8 • $15.95

Open Secret

In poetry, dialogs, epigrams, and essays, the author addresses our illusions concerning the mind, the self, logic, time, space, and causation, and gives his own substantial interpretation of The Heart Sutra.

ISBN 1-59181-014-0 • $15.95

Unworldly Wise

Wu Wei's final book is an enlightened parable in the form of a conversation between a wise owl and a naïve rabbit about God, friendship, loneliness, and religion.

ISBN 1-59181-019-1 • $12.95

Sentient Publications, LLC publishes books on cultural creativity, experimental education, transformative spirituality, holistic health, new science, and ecology, approached from an integral viewpoint. Our authors are intensely interested in exploring the nature of life from fresh perspectives, addressing life's great questions, and fostering the full expression of the human potential. Sentient Publications' books arise from the spirit of inquiry and the richness of the inherent dialogue between writer and reader.

We are very interested in hearing from our readers. To direct suggestions or comments to us, or to be added to our mailing list, please contact:

SENTIENT PUBLICATIONS, LLC

1113 Spruce Street
Boulder, CO 80302
303.443.2188
contact@sentientpublications.com
www.sentientpublications.com